The Branded Man

Cordy Lowell lost more than his youth and his horse when they branded him, but the red-hot branding iron did more than just scar his chest, it forged a strong thirst for revenge.

Taking sides in a range war, Cordy found himself fighting on the side of a wheelchair-bound ranch owner against Bosewell, a greedy man who wasn't satisfied with owning most of the basin, getting rich from his cattle and horse breeding operation. It wasn't long before the fight became personal and Cordy had a chance to find retribution. If he lived long enough. . . .

The Branded Man

J.D. Ryder

A Black Horse Western

ROBERT HALE · LONDON

© William Sheehy 2009
First published in Great Britain 2009

ISBN 978-0-7090-8838-7

Robert Hale Limited
Clerkenwell House
Clerkenwell Green
London EC1R 0HT

www.halebooks.com

Typeset by
Derek Doyle & Associates, Shaw Heath
Printed and bound in Great Britain by
CPI Antony Rowe, Chippenham and Eastbourne

CHAPTER ONE

Hearing the long drawn out scream, the young rider's head came up with a snap. He pulled his horse to a stop and sat listening, trying to figure out where the sound had come from. For a few minutes he didn't move. The horse, taking advantage of the halt, reached out to pull a mouthful of summer-dried grass.

Cordy Lowell had been riding, slumped in his saddle just like any tired old man would. But Cordy Lowell was young; he hadn't even started to shave regularly yet. For a long moment he sat his saddle. Then, not hearing anything but the soft movement of a breeze moving through the underbrush, he relaxed, letting his mind go back to the state of bewilderment it had been in for these past days.

He had given up trying to figure out what he could have done. It was too late and he had been helpless about it anyway. With his chin resting on his chest, his eyes staring blankly at the long black mane of his horse, he sat as he had before hearing what he thought had been a scream.

About to give the horse a touch of his heel, he was just lifting the reins when it came again, a shriek of unquestionable pain that climbed until losing itself in a fading whimper. Someone was in deep trouble.

Cordy kneed the horse forward and reined a little to the left, the direction the sound had come from. Stroking the side of his horse with a heel, he pushed the animal into a trot.

Cordy had been there when his horse was foaled. He had actually helped his pa's favorite mare with the birthing. Waiting until it grew big enough to carry the boy had been hard but worth it. A dun, the horse was a pale gray color that looked even lighter against the pure black mane and tail and a wide stripe of the same hue down the back. A brush stroke of light spots across the rump was the only sign of there being Appaloosa blood mixed in. From the first time he rode the horse, the two had been inseparable. It reacted instantly to the boy's boot heel.

As he crested the next ridge top Cordy pulled up, almost running headlong into the group of men bunched around something on the ground. Before he could react, one of the men bellowed out an order and the boy was pulled from the saddle. For a brief minute he fought against the rough hands that held him, but stopped when he saw the men lying on the ground. Cordy froze at what he saw. Tied spread-eagled in the dirt were two men, their shirts torn away and their pale white chests bare to the hot afternoon sun. Smoke rose in a soft swirl from the wound on one chest while the other man's body heaved in an attempt to break free of the bindings.

'Well, don't just stand there,' a hard, coarse, nasally voice ordered. 'Get on with it.'

Movement to one side caught Cordy's attention and he watched, unable to move, as a shabbily dressed cowboy, his hands protected by thick leather gloves, ran from a small fire holding a branding-iron. Without stopping, the white-hot iron was hard-pressed against the bound man's bare chest. The scream that broke from the man's throat was gut-wrenching. Cordy felt his legs start to give away but was roughly jerked to his feet by the hands that had seized him.

Not able to tear his eyes away, Cordy watched as the branded man's body twisted against the ropes holding him down. Whimpering cries had replaced the roar of pain, and these faded to a soft mewing sound before dying away completely.

Yanked around, Cordy found himself being looked over by the tall lanky man who had given the order.

'Well, what in tarnation do we have here?'

The man scowled, his eyes partly hidden under heavy brows that almost met in the middle, a gash of a mouth twisted into a permanent sneer by a white scar that ran from his whiskered chin across one cheek.

'He came busting in while you and the Injun were having your fun with that rustler, Price', the man holding Cordy said hoarsely.

'Came busting in, huh?' the leader, Price, snarled. 'Wal, it's probably a good lesson for the boy to learn. See that,' Price pointed at the two men lying motionless on the ground, 'that's what happens whenever we catch someone rustling our beef. Hangin's too good for their kind. And too quick for them, I figure. Laying a brand on them is sure to learn them the error of their ways.' Price chuckled, a humorless sound, Cordy thought. 'Anyway, the Injun likes to put a hot iron to them that I say deserve it.'

Cordy glanced over at the ragged cowboy standing off by the fire, holding the cooling branding-iron in one hand. Long dirty black braids hung down each side of his square head. Two coal-black eyes stared back at the boy.

'Say,' Price's voice took on a sound of wonderment, 'that's a good-looking animal standing there. Caleb, toss your rope on that hoss. Let's take a closer look-see.'

'That's my horse. You keep your hands off him,' Cordy yelled, struggling to get free. The man holding him laughed and letting go with one hand hit the boy on the side of his head, knocking Cordy to the ground. For a few minutes he lay where he had fallen, holding his head in both hands, his vision blurry and his ears ringing. Slowly, as the fog that filled his skull started to ease he heard the man named Price talking.

'Will you looky here,' he heard Price's nasally voice cutting through the confusion as things came slowly into focus. One cowboy was holding his horse by the headgear while Price ran his hands gently down each leg, feeling the lean strength.

'Now, this is a horse, gentlemen. One that'll run all day and still be ahead of whatever's chasing you.' Price finished walking around Cordy's horse and patted the animal almost tenderly on the spotted rump. Looking down at the young man he lifted the other side of his mouth in what was probably met to be a smile.

'Wal, boys, you know what I think we got ourselves here?' When nobody answered, Price laughed. 'A horse thief, that's what. Ain't no young'n like him gonna be riding such a fine animal as is this 'un. Nosiree, boys, I'd say we got us a real boss-thief. Yeah, a little young for it, I'll admit, but what else could it be?'

'I ain't no thief,' Cordy yelled out, his voice sounding to his ears like an echo rattling around in his head. 'That's my horse. I raised him myself.' Rolling over he raised himself to his hands and knees, letting his head hang down as dizziness made his world spin.

Price laughed. 'Oh, and I'm suppose to believe you? Not likely. This fine animal ain't even got a brand on him. Not a mark that shows he belongs to anyone. Why, if'n I was to put my brand on him, it'd be my horse, now wouldn't it?' He glanced over at the Indian and nodded.

'Stick that little brand in the fire, No-nose. Let's make this all legal, like.'

A faint smile creased the Indian's bronze face as he toed an iron into the middle of the small fire.

Cordy shook his head and tried to gain his feet, only to have someone clout him on the chin, knocking him flat on his back in the dirt.

'Hey, Price,' he heard someone say from a long way away. 'This isn't exactly kosher. Stealing the boy's animal is, well, it's stealing.'

'Caleb, you're kinda new to the ranch,' Cordy heard Price's voice, 'so I'll let it pass this time. But don't let it happen again, you hear me? I'm the one what says who's a rustler and who isn't. This horse is too good for a young'n like this one. Why, he ain't so smart hisself. Coming in where he ain't got no business. As I said, without any mark on it anywheres, who's to say who it belongs to?

Hurry up with that iron, No-nose.'

Another voice, softer but coming from somewhere else cut in.

'Better not put your stamp on that horse, Price. What'd ya think the old man'll say if'n he was to hear how it came to be wearing your brand? You know how he likes fine-looking animals. He'll want that horse for hisself and when he finds out how you got it, he'll be pissed.'

For what Cordy thought was a long time nobody said anything. Slowly, as the darkness faded and he tried to raise his head, he let out a groan. Rolling over, he tried to see what was happening.

'You might be right,' Price snarled. 'Ah, hell with it. Go ahead, No-nose. Use the ranch iron to brand the horse. We'll take it in to the old man and tell him how we found it running free as a breeze. You got that everyone? Running free as the breeze.'

Cordy heard various grunts as the hands signaled their agreement. He watched as the Indian, frowning, pushed another branding-iron into the center of the fire.

Shaking his head gently, Cordy tried to think of a way to stop his horse from being stolen. As the fuzziness once again left his mind, he found himself close to crying with frustration. Gritting his teeth, he clinched his jaw. He would not cry. He was not a baby.

'Now, somehow it ain't fair,' Price said, laughing again. 'Old No-nose John was looking forward to putting my brand on the horse. It ain't the same for him as having to put the ranch brand on it. I tell you, boys, this is one Indian who thinks the sun shines only for me and I hate to cause him to lose out of his being able to make me happy. So I'll tell ya what. Heat up that little iron of mine, No-nose.'

'What ya gonna do, boss?' someone asked.

'Why, we got us a horse-thief, don't we? And we all know how No-nose likes to put the hot iron to rustlers and horse-thieves. We're gonna make this boy think twice before ever trying to steal another horse. Old No-nose is gonna put my mark on him. Now, rip that shirt off his skinny chest.'

Realizing what he'd just heard, Cordy kicked out and tried to crawl away only to be held down by two or three of the cowboys.

'Hurry it up, Injun,' someone called, 'we can't hold him like this for long. He's wiggling like a stomped-on snake left too long in the sun.'

Cordy yelled, remembering the screams he'd heard earlier. Twisting and kicking he thrashed about, struggling to get free. Hearing a grunt, he looked up as the Indian, holding the red-hot iron, kneeled over him. Shoving his knee into the boy's stomach, Cordy thought he saw the man smile but whipped his eyes back to the branding-iron as it pressed against his bare skin.

The scream he heard was as loud and piercing as those of the other two men. Blackness swept in as the stabbing pain seared his body. The shriek he was hearing, he knew, was his own, fading only as he lost consciousness.

15

CHAPTER TWO

The tall, long-limbed cowboy sat tiredly slumped in the second-hand saddle that had come with his chestnut gelding, looking down at a group of ranch buildings. He rolled a smoke, a habit he'd picked up somewhere along the way, and looked down at the outfit below.

It was a likely-looking spread, a lot bigger and better than his pa's horse-breeding ranch. Thinking about the place his pa had built brought back a lot of bad memories. Memories he thought he'd buried a long time ago.

'You know, horse,' he said, just to be talking, 'I helped bury Ma and then I had to bury Pa right there next to her. I can't clearly recall what they looked like, but I sure remember the look on that sheriff's face when he came out there to tell me to get off the place.'

The elder Lowell had been digging fence-post holes when he was snake-bit. It took most of a week for him to die and it wasn't but a week or two later that the lawman and another man had ridden in.

'Hell's fire, there I was just a boy and not knowing anything about such matters. They showed me some papers saying how Pa owed money and the place would have to be sold to pay it back.' The horse didn't act like it'd heard, simply dropped its head to pull at a bit of dried grass.

'Yeah, they told me to pack what I wanted and to get gone. All I rode out with was the clothes on my back, that grainy black-and-white daguerreotype portrait of Ma and Pa taken on their wedding day and my horse. And then someone came along and stole that horse from me. Well, that's one thing we'll get back. But I gotta tell you, it's sure unlikely I'll ever have anything like that place down there.'

Pulling the smoke deep into his lungs he grimaced. Damn, it'd be good to get a full night's sleep, come awake in the morning feeling strong and alive. He couldn't remember the last time he'd felt like that. Well, he frowned, yes he could. It'd been while he was back in the mountains with Zeb and Cletus. Those two old-timers had become his family, first helping his body get well and then working to heal his mind.

Unconscious of doing it, his left palm lightly brushed the front of his trail-dusty shirt. The two old men had done what they could, nursing him back to health, then teaching him all that he knew. They had shared everything they had with him but they couldn't erase the mark that burned clear to his soul. Maybe down there at that ranch he'd find what he was searching for. If not, then maybe the next one. Possibly, when it was all over, he'd be able to get the rest he needed.

*

19

Coming out of the high country, after Zeb had died and Cletus rode on south, he'd hired on with a large cattle operation, working a couple months helping with a spring round-up. Dirty work, chousing cattle out of the scrub, but the time had gone by fast and he'd learned a lot about the contrariness of the beasts. Another season had been spent helping build fences on another spread. That had set the pattern. Over the next few years he'd gone from one ranch to the next. Nobody had offered him a permanent job and he wouldn't have taken it if they had. He still had a horse to find and a man to kill.

He rarely removed his shirt, but each time he did he saw the brand burned into his chest. It strengthened his resolve. All he could recall was a name, Price. He thought that was enough.

'Silver Canyon is the place,' he'd been told when drawing his last pay from the rancher at the end of that round-up. ' 'Most everyone's heading down that way. Started out, it was just another tent city built up near to a gold strike.

Turned out not to be much gold though, and all the get-rich-quick folk moved on. Was a few what stayed. Nowadays it's the center of commerce for that region. A number of cattle outfits and even a couple small silver mines make it a likely place for a young buck to make his fortune. You won't go wrong there, I reckon.'

Looking over the outfit down below was likely one of those cattle ranches he'd been told about. If so, he might be able to hire on.

He wasn't really looking for work but the money in his pocket or even the gold left in the little leather poke hidden in his saddlebags wouldn't last for ever. Anyway, he'd find out more as a working cowhand than as just another saddle tramp. Nobody would pay him any attention if he was riding for the brand while he was looking to see if his dun horse and the man named Price were in this part of the country.

Relaxing for another long minute he continued to look the place over.

The main house sat a little higher than the

other buildings. A series of barns and corrals lay off in a cluster to the left and a long bunkhouse and more corrals could be seen on the other side of the big ranch yard. Cordy liked the looks of it all. It had signs that the owners cared, that things were in good repair. The ranch house itself was all white-painted with some dark paint covering the shutters hanging on each side of the numerous windows. From where he sat he could see that a covered veranda ran across the front and along the near side. Four horses were tied to a hitch rail in front.

He pinched out the burning end of his quirley, touched the chestnut's flank with a heel and made his way down the brushy slope toward the house. A few clumps of trees, mostly pines and down near the bottom a couple old oaks, forced the trail he was on to circle around. The trail, no more than a thin animal track, brought him onto the flats behind the largest barn. Hearing loud voices as he neared the corner of the barn he reined back. He didn't want to ride in and interrupt a private discussion.

'Damn it, Colfield, I made my offer in good faith. It's a fair offer, too. Look at you, a sick old man who can't keep enough hands on the place to make a decent round-up. Sooner or later you're going to have to face it, keep going like you are and the bank'll take over. My offer won't go on much longer. I got my own ranch to run.' A man snarled over his shoulder as he came down the steps. Cordy watched as the squat barrel of a man with thick black hair worn slicked back with some kind of pomade carefully adjusted his wide-brimmed hat before jerking free the reins of a horse.

The man's voice coming from the porch had a weakness. 'Your offer isn't anyway near what this place is worth, Bosewell, and you know it.'

'Not without enough men to work it, it ain't worth spit.'

Cordy caught movement and watched as three men, cowhands from the way they moved and the clothes on their backs, moved around the end of the porch and stepped onto their horses, to sit their saddles behind the loud-mouthed man.

'Don't think Hannah and I are through,' the man on the porch's shadow went on. 'We've sent outside for men, men who won't be frightened off by your high-handed threats.'

The other man laughed as he grabbed the horn and swung into the saddle. The other three mounted men spread out on each side.

'I've made no threats. The men around here know enough not to get in the middle of things, that's all. They know better. And as far as anyone coming from outside the basin, don't bank on it. I'm not all that sure the telegraph lines weren't down recently. Seems I was told a lot of outgoing telegrams didn't get sent out.'

Chuckling, the leader of the mounted men reined around only to pull back abruptly when seeing Cordy sitting his horse next to the barn.

'What the hell . . . What're you doing,

sitting there?' he snorted letting his hand fall on the butt of his holstered revolver.

Wishing he'd thought to have his rifle ready, Cordy merely smiled as he thumbed the thong holding his Colt in its holster. He still had his pa's old Starr revolver in his saddlebags but when Zeb had died he'd wrapped the old man's Colt around his waist. The old-timer's Henry was in the saddle scabbard under his left leg.

'Why, hearing you laugh at and threaten another man made me wonder. Personally I didn't think much of what I heard at all.'

'This ain't none of your business and you'd do well to keep out of it.'

'Well,' Cordy let his tone harden, become more menacing. He kneed his gelding a step or two closer, pushing. 'I reckon you're right. But as I might be hiring on here, I did find what was said interesting.'

'You don't seem to be able to count,' the big man snarled. 'There're four of us.'

'Yep, I can count. But I figure those others there don't matter much. I'm betting before you can pull that pistol you're wearing I've already put my bullet right in the center of that fat gut of yours. Now then, those hired hands sitting behind you will have a hard time getting paid if you're dead, won't they?' Raising his voice a little but not taking his eyes off the boss man, he called out. 'Something to think about, boys.'

Nobody moved for a long moment, before Bosewell, using both hands to lift his horse's reins, laughed humorlessly. 'I don't know what you think you heard just now but you'll be a lot better off if you keep riding. This ranch is a hard-luck spread.' Turning his head to the side he called to his men, 'C'mon, let's get the hell out of here.'

Cordy heeled his horse out a few feet more, turning to watch the four horsemen ride away. Reining back toward the house, he stopped as a young woman stepped into the sunshine. She wasn't, he saw, a real pretty woman, but her hair hanging down each side of her face seemed to sparkle a little in the bright light.

'Ma'am,' he stammered, 'I apologize for cutting in like that. I certainly didn't mean to eavesdrop on your conversation or to cause trouble with your guest.'

'That man was not a guest.' Her voice had steel in it. 'My father and I thank you for being there and taking part. Bosewell owns the B-Bar-B Cattle Company. It's the biggest spread in the whole basin and he thinks he can do anything he wants. So far he's been able to, even to the point of forcing people to sell whether they want to or not.'

'Hannah, this man isn't interested in our problems,' the man who was still in the porch's shadow cut in, 'but we do thank you, stranger.'

'Father, you heard him. He said he may be hiring on. It's best if he knows what he'd be getting involved with, wouldn't it?' Turning back toward Cordy she shaded her eyes with one hand. 'Were you serious about hiring on? Are you here in answer to the telegram I sent last week?'

'Well, ma'am,' Cordy smiled and let both of

his hands rest on the saddle horn, 'I am looking for work, but no, I didn't get any invite from the telegraph office.'

'Daughter, didn't you hear Bosewell? He's done something, probably scared that old man at the telegraph office into not sending your telegram.'

'What is it this Bosewell wants? Your ranch?'

'He's just plain greedy and wants to own the entire basin,' the woman snapped. 'Already two or three of the smaller ranchers have sold out and moved on. Now he's going for the bigger ones, like ours. Thinks he can do what he wants and has hired a bunch of fast gunmen to help him do it.'

'I take it he has a cattle ranch?'

'Well, now he does. On B-Bar-B range he raises horses. He came into the valley with a small herd of cattle but then he brought in a prize stud horse, sold off all his beeves and went to breeding horses on that range. Since taking over the Lazy R, though, he's shipping cattle again.'

Cordy felt sweat bead his forehead. 'What

kind of prize horse are you talking about?'

'Oh, it's a beauty.' The man on the porch wheeled out next to his daughter. Cordy saw that his chair had two large wheels in the back and a smaller one in front. 'Anyone knows anything about horseflesh can see this is a special animal. A dun, the horse is a light silvery-gray color with a pure black mane and tail and a wide stripe of the same hue down its back. Bosewell used to ride that horse a lot and loved to show it off. Now though, the animal is too valuable to ride and is used only as breeding stock. You stay around the area long and you'll see a lot of its offspring. You can be sure of the parentage by the brush-stroke of light spots across its rump. The dun certainly had some Appaloosa blood mixed in somewhere along the way. It's a beauty.'

Cordy felt his head spin. His pa had bred that horse from a tiger dun he owned and an Appaloosa dam he'd traded for from a traveling medicine man. His horse, the horse stolen from him had shown markings from that mating. He had found his horse.

CHAPTER THREE

'Were you serious about hiring on?' asked the old man looking up at Cordy from his wheelchair.

'Yep, sure am. My name's Cordy Lowell.'

'I'm Zachariah Colfield and this is my daughter, Hannah. What we got here is what should be a pretty good spread. Been running a couple thousand head, mostly a mix of Texas Longhorn and a white faced shorthorn. Good beef and the range is good.'

'But. . . ?' Cordy didn't finish the question.

'Yeah, but. But where last year we ran a good-sized herd down to the railhead, this year we ain't got the men to make a round-up.'

'Tell him everything, Father, it's only fair that he knows what we're facing.' Hannah Colfield was slender-built with her high-waisted dress verifying her young womanhood. Long brown hair hung down over both shoulders, ending in soft waves and curls. Cordy liked the way her eyes flashed with anger as she explained. He felt good just looking at her but tore his gaze away before it became obvious.

'Wal, daughter, you may be right. Alright, Mr Lowell, here it is. A couple years ago I borrowed money from the bank in Silver Canyon. Used it to put in a three-strand barbed-wire fence all along our southwest border. Good thing we did too, seeing as how that fool Bosewell somehow got title to Rodgers' Lazy R last fall. Well, Carl tells me that most of the fencing out along that end of the range is all down. Never had no problems with old man Rodgers in all the time we been here. Not like that now, not since Boswell took over the Lazy R. Guess that'd be the first thing to do, rebuild all that fencing.'

'If you're hiring me, you can't keep calling

me mister anything. Name's Cordy. You say Carl told you the fence is all down. Who is Carl?'

'He's the only hand we've got left,' Hannah said. 'Carl's been with us since Father and Mother first came into the basin. He's almost like one of the family.'

The elder Colfield snorted gently. 'Girl, he's been my best friend since long before you was born. Fact is,' he said, looking up at Cordy, who was still in the saddle, 'Hannah here usually calls him Uncle Carl. I guess because he's old that fool Bosewell has left him alone. I don't know.'

'If the fence is down, then there will likely be a lot of Bosewell's stock mixed in with your beeves. That'll mean pushing them back. And from what you're saying, the only hands on the place are Carl and me.'

'I can ride,' said Hannah strongly, 'and my pinto is a good cutting horse. So there are three of us.'

'Now, girl, I don't want you getting hurt,' her father argued. 'Mr Lowell, that ain't all.

That bank note is coming due. Now if we can make up a herd, the market is up and the note won't be a problem. But if Bosewell stops me from hiring enough hands, then having the fence down won't make no difference.'

Carl Hanson could have been fifty or seventy, it was impossible for Cordy to judge. The older man's face and hands were bronzed from having been out in the sun most of his life. When he took his hat off the rest of his forehead was pale white. Wrinkles along that forehead and spreading out from his pale-blue eyes were many and deep. Cordy was taken by the whiteness of his teeth when he smiled, and that was his usual expression: a big toothy smile.

'Wal there, young man, I sure do welcome you. I was getting tired of being all alone in this bunkhouse. Do you play cribbage? I do like a good game of crib come evening time.'

Cordy had to laugh. 'Yeah, me'n Pa used to play some after supper.'

'Good, good. Now you go ahead and throw

your bedroll on anyone of them bunks there.' He waved down the long, high-raftered bunkhouse. A row of bunk beds lined both walls with a pot-bellied iron stove sitting in the middle. It was clear which bunk was Carl's, it was the only one made up. Cordy tossed his bedroll and saddle bags on a bunk some distance further down the line, on the other side of the stove.

'Miss Hannah'll be bringing out a pile of blankets for ya, I 'xpect. She's a good one, all right. Takes good care of her pa, does all the cooking and keeping the home place in good shape. Pains me a lot to see the trouble her and her pa's in, though. Purely does.'

'What happened to her father to put him in that wheelchair?'

'Ah, you'd never guess it to see him now, but he was a good-sized man once. I grew up on the Colfield ranch down along the Texas panhandle. Grew up with him and his brother, two peas in a pod, they was. Zachariah don't talk much about his brother. He just took off one morning, said he was going to look at the world, leaving Zachariah to take care of his ma and pa. Wal, old man Colfield's ranch wasn't much; hard scrabble, you might say. A lotta years we fought to make it there, but the cholera got 'em all, my pa and ma and Zach's too. We buried them there and headed north. Got here with a couple hundred head and staked out the Boxed C. Zach married up a few years later and things was going good, until his wife died giving birth to Hannah.'

'How come you didn't stake out a spread?' Cordy asked and then stopped, holding up a hand. 'No, that isn't any of my business. Sorry I asked.'

'Wal, no harm done. Truth to tell I ain't got the drive to take on owning a ranch. I can work hard but don't want the responsibility, you know? Look at it, Zach has the Boxed C but he ain't so happy, now is he? Nope, better I say, to have my place here in the bunkhouse.'

Cordy, thinking back to the troubles his pa had had, nearly agreed with him.

'Anyway, it was a horse Zach was breaking what fell back on him. Broke something inside. Hasn't been able to walk or sit a saddle since.'

'The boss told me about the fence being knocked down.'

'Yeah. Knocked down and the bob-wire cut. That lets Lazy R cows roam all over the place. Wouldn't've happened when Rodgers owned the spread, but Bosewell, it's likely it was his crew what pulled the fence down.'

'That doesn't sound very neighborly.' Cordy frowned before going on. 'And he's stopping anyone from hiring on here?'

'Seems like it. Don't know but what that's going to bring an end to the Boxed C.'

'Any law in Silver Canyon?'

'Yep, a sheriff. All elected and a good man, from what I can see. Excepting that he knows which side of his bread the butter is on. Says there's little if anything he can do. Don't know what'll happen to Zach and Hannah if they lose the ranch. Don't know what I'll do either.'

'Guess we'll have to do what we can to make

that not happen, then, won't we?'

'What can we do? Me, I'm an old man about reaching the end of my string. You could likely do what needs to get done, but not by your ownself.' Waving at the gunbelt hanging around Cordy's waist, he continued, 'I reckon you'd have to use that pistol, too. And that'd likely get you killed. Bosewell's got himself a handful of bad asses and his foreman is one tough hombre. Don't want to scare you off before you get a meal behind your belt, but you gotta know what you'd be facing. That man Price is bad enough. The others only make it impossible.'

'What's his name?'

'Price? He's a big man and mean. Been foreman for the B-Bar-B Cattle Company since Bosewell came into the basin ten years or so ago. A real bad one, he is.'

Price. Cordy couldn't believe there could be two men with that name anywhere in this part of the country, the same country where his dun had ended up. It had to be his dun and it had to be the man who had branded him.

CHAPTER FOUR

Carl and Cordy were roping horses from the biggest of the stock corrals the next morning when Hannah, dressed in pants, riding-boots and a long-sleeved shirt came striding across the yard.

'Saddle a horse for me, will you?'

'Sure will, Miss Hannah.' Carl nodded, a big smile creasing his face.

Cordy looked up from tightening the cinches on his saddle. 'You riding out with us this morning?'

'Yes, I'd like to see the damage to our fence for myself. Maybe it isn't as bad as Carl said it was.'

'Well, we can certainly hope for the best.'

Carl had shoved wire-cutters and heavy gloves in his saddle bags and Cordy was carrying a shovel and a steel bar.

As they rode at a fast walk across the rolling range, Carl and Hannah pointed out landmarks, showing Cordy the Boxed C property. A series of spring-fed waterholes had been cleared out, Hannah explained, when her father had first staked out his boundaries.

'We had half a dozen hands year round those first few years. They dug out the waterholes and put in rock dams on some of the creeks running through the range. What with the winters we get and the ponds to hold back the spring run-off, water has never been a problem.'

'Mostly,' Carl said at one point, 'we can get by now with a few men year round and need to hire extra only during the branding and culling or when we're moving a herd to the railhead. Wintertime it takes just two or three men to ride the back range, keeping the fool cattle out of trouble. That is when we can fmd the men to hire.'

Nobody had anything to say about that. All through the morning's ride they passed bunches of cattle, mostly brown in color, either lying calmly chewing their cuds or simply browsing the short spring grasses. Cordy noticed that the shorthorn breeding made the cattle heavier than the taller, thinner longhorn. Most of the clusters showed this blend with only a few of the animals having with the wide needle-sharp horns. It was easy to see that the range was close to being overgrazed, a round-up and culling was certainly called for.

The first they saw of the fence was a ragged line of wood posts, some with wire hanging down and others leaning at crazy angles from being pushed over. Corl and Cordy reined back and took time to roll their smokes as they looked over the damage.

'Well,' Cordy said after studying the destruction that stretched in the distance out of sight, 'I'd say we're back to rebuilding the entire length. At least from what we can see from here. But some of those posts look to be still in good shape and the holes won't have to be dug again, so it isn't as bad as it could be.'

'But it'll take us a long time to do the job. Father had a lot of hands working when we strung that fence. The three of us, it'll take the rest of the summer.'

'And there's still the round-up to get done,' said Cordy. 'I don't want to talk out of turn, but it looks to me that the thing to do is go get a few men out here. Say five or six to string the fence and that many more to get started on cutting and branding.'

'Where are you going to find that many men who'll come to work for us? Bosewell and his gunmen have scared everyone away.'

Cordy nodded. 'So I've been told. But what if I went ahead and rode in to send the telegram to Denver? Shoot, it probably wouldn't hurt for me to ride on over to the big city myself. Is there a stage line operating between Silver Canyon and Denver?'

'Better'n that,' Carl said. 'We got us a train. Runs out in the afternoon and comes back the next morning. I've taken it a couple times, gone over to Denver for a drink or two. I believe in spreading my money around, you know?'

Cordy and Hannah had to laugh.

'Yes, that makes sense, I suppose. But I kinda think someone should hang close to the ranch. Way I see it, Bosewell won't like it if he finds out what I'm doing. He just might decide to come back out to cause some trouble. That'll be your job, Carl. Sit with a rifle, standing guard.'

Hannah nodded, reaching across to touch the old man's hand. 'He's right. I know Father and I will both feel better if we know you are there, Carl.'

'After all this is over, Carl,' Cordy chuckled, 'however things work out, I'll take you for a train ride myself. And the first drink is on me.'

Having got directions into town and the name of the man to contact in Denver, Cordy changed into his last clean shirt and rode the ten miles or so into Silver Canyon. Just as had been described to him, the town sat on both sides of a deep valley with the main business section at a wide place at the south end. As he rode down the main street he could see a steam engine with a string of cars hooked on at the far end. Somewhere down there, he figured, would be the telegraph office.

He hadn't decided whether or not to send a telegram offering employment. It'd be a lot easier than spending the rest of the day and the night doing the job in person. First, though, he wanted to talk with the sheriff.

He took his time and looked the town over as he walked his pony down the street. He pulled in when he saw the sign hanging over a door saying it was the jail and sheriff's office.

'What can I do for ya, stranger?' The old man sitting behind the desk looked up when Cordy pushed though the door.

'Looking for the sheriff.'

'What for? You got some kind of problem?'

'Are you the sheriff?'

'Wal, no. But anything I can do for ya might

save him the trouble, ya see?'

Cordy chuckled. 'Nope. What business I've got is with the big chief himself, not the jailer.'

'Wal, I never.' The man slapped the top of the desk in frustration.

'Don't know where he is, is that it?'

'I most certainly do. This time of day he's likely over at the general store gossiping with old Harold Peeves what owns it. So there, I do know where he is.'

'Guess that's where I'll go, then. Thanks, old-timer.'

Cordy smiled and shut the door on the grumbling man. He left his horse tied to the rail and stood looking first one way then the other for the store. He spotted it directly across the street.

A tiny bell jingled as he pushed open the screen door and stepped into the darkness. Waiting for his eyes to adjust, he stood just inside enjoying the smells of leather, soap, cheese and all the other things the store carried.

'Help you there?' one of the two men

standing at a counter over along one wall called out. A third man was at a table further back, looking through a pile of shirts stacked there.

'Looking for the sheriff. Old man over at the jail said I'd likely find him here.'

Both men laughed. 'And I bet he's madder than hell if you didn't tell him what you wanted to see me about. Rufus is one of the biggest gossips in town and he purely hates it to be left out of things. I'm the sheriff, Sheriff Claude Dallas, by name. Now, what can I do for you?'

'Nothing for me, exactly. I just hired on out at the Boxed C, the Colfield place. Seems they're having some trouble with another rancher here in the basin. I happened to overhear one man, a Mr Bosewell, tell Mr Colfield that he'd stopped a telegram from going out. Seems Bosewell is also making it difficult for the Boxed C to hire hands. Anything you can enlighten me on about all this?'

'Yeah, I can. It's real simple. Bosewell is the

big auger around here. It's his payroll that keeps this town alive. Now you see how it is. Ain't much anyone can do, either. He's got the money to hire and the men he's been hiring aren't to be fooled with. That's the way the stick floats.'

'What I hear is that one man is running the show 'cause he's the richest. I was told he got that way by running other ranchers out. Don't you think this would be a better town if there were a dozen ranchers and their payrolls rather than just one?'

'Look stranger, in a better world that's reasonable, but it's not like that here and now. Mr Bosewell is running things. Folks like the Colfields, they're good people but even when left alone he only hires six or eight men. Bosewell has been buying up a lot of the little spreads and he's got – what do you think, Harold, thirty or forty men? And guess where they spend all their money? Right here in downtown Silver Canyon. Sad to say, but that's the way it is and there ain't no one gonna take sides against him. It's his money that pays to keep most of these businesses here in town worthwhile. If I was you, I'd think again about trying to buck him.'

'Sheriff, you were elected by the people of this area, not just one rancher. Don't you think you have a duty to everyone? Not just the biggest wolf in the bunch?'

'Yeah, you're right, they all voted me in. But the town people got the most votes, a lot more'n the few ranchers that's left and guess outa whose pocket the most money comes to pay my wages?' Both men chuckled.

'I guess I can see your point, Sheriff. Sooner or later, though, that kind of situation is sure to cause you all some trouble, don't you think?'

'Nothing I can't handle. And if I can't, then there're all those gunnies Mr Bosewell has out at the B-Bar-B. Things are pretty well under control, I'd say.'

Cordy nodded. 'Well, I hope you're right. By the way, my name is Cordy Lowell and I'd appreciate it if you'd spread the word around that the Boxed C is hiring.'

'Won't do you any good, Lowell. Ain't nobody gonna buck Mr Bosewell. And here's a little advice, don't go pushing it. If Mr Bosewell says nobody'll work for old man Colfield, then nobody will. Best you get back on your horse and keep riding.'

Cordy smiled but let his words grow hard. 'Nope, can't do that. Got some men to hire, some fence to mend and some cattle to sell. Sheriff, I'd say that trouble is heading your way, not sooner or later but starting today. It's too bad, but there it is.' He touched the brim of his hat, nodded and stepped back out into the sunshine.

He stopped on the sidewalk and settled the holstered Colt on his hip. His horse and his man were somewhere in this basin, so he wouldn't be riding on. Not yet, anyhow. Thinking of the pot he was stirring and how that should lead him to a man named Price made him feel good inside. The best he'd felt in a long time.

CHAPTER FIVE

'Hey, stranger, you got a minute?'

Cordy stepped quickly aside as he turned back toward the door, pulling his Colt half out of the leather. Seeing it was the man who had been looking at shirts standing there, his hands open and away from his body, Cordy let the pistol drop back in place.

'Man, it isn't a good idea to come up behind a fella like that. Especially not after the fella's been told off by the local law.'

'I reckon you're right. From what I overheard you're heading for a lot of trouble less'n you give it up and ride out.'

'And that's not likely. So, what do you want?'

'A job. A riding job.'

The man certainly didn't look like he was a hand. Looking him over, Cordy took in his shabby flat-heeled boots, a pair of pants that most likely was once part of a Sunday-go-to-meeting suit and a dingy suit coat that didn't match the pants. The need of a shave and a haircut, and probably a few good meals made the man look older than he likely was. Cordy thought the man was only a few years older than he was.

'Yeah, I know I don't look it, but times have been tough lately. Until a year or so ago I was a rider working out at the Lazy R. Before that I rode for Bosewell's B-Bar-B. When that greedy son bought out Rodgers, I got fired. Been doing anything I could find since, that means mostly swamping out the saloon.'

'How come Bosewell was able to fire you?'

'I didn't like a lot of things that foreman, Price, was doing. This was a good town, had a bunch of little farmers and cow outfits around until that crowd showed up. It looked good, going to work for a big spread like what

Bosewell put together. Good pay, better than anyone else was able to offer. But, well, some of the things that went on didn't sit well with me. Price ran me off and so I went over to the Lazy R and worked there for a time. Then when Rodgers sold his spread I knew what would happen so I rode out. Been looking for work, real work, ever since.'

'And you heard I was looking to hire a crew for the Boxed C?'

'Yeah.'

Cordy nodded slowly. He had to start somewhere and he knew he'd be taking a chance on anyone he'd find locally. 'All right. I'm Cordy Lowell. I'll write a note for you to give to Mr Colfield. He can decide whether or not to put you on. C'mon, I'm heading down to the telegraph office.'

'I answer to Caleb, Mr Lowell and thanks.'

'Not mister anything, Caleb, just Cordy. The only mister on the place is Mr Colfield.'

Neither man spoke as they walked down the street toward the railroad station. They stepped up onto the platform and Cordy went into the ticket office with Caleb right behind. Hardwood benches lined two of the walls of the waiting-room, with a few spindly-looking chairs scattered here and there across the bare wood floor. A counter took up the far wall. Behind that barrier a man wearing a black leather visor sat at a desk, hunched over a clicking telegraph. The two men stepped up to the counter and waited as the operator, writing something on a form as fast as he could, finished taking the message.

Cordy spotted a pad of telegram blanks on the counter. He wet the end of a lead pencil and quickly wrote out his message. At last, after fingering the telegraph key with some finality, the man stood and came over to the counter.

'Yes, sir, something I can do for you?' The telegraph operator was a small, skinny man, about a foot shorter than Cordy. He had to tilt his head up in order to look into the young man's face. Glaring up at Cordy from under the visor he frowned. 'Want to send a telegram?' he demanded.

Cordy smiled. 'Yeah. I've written it out and here's the name of the man to send it to.'

The operator quickly read the brief note, his frown deepening.

'Alright. Cost you a dollar.'

Cordy nodded and dug a coin out of his pants pocket.

The operator put the message aside and looked back at his customer. 'Wal, you want something else?'

'Yes, I want to see you send that message.'

'I'll do it in a minute. Got to wait for the line to clear.'

'That's not good enough.' Cordy pulled his Colt, thumbed back on the hammer and used the barrel to push back his Stetson. He let his smile fade. 'I want to hear that message go out, now. And be careful, I know the code and it would be disappointing to hear something other than what I wrote going out.'

'You can't do that, coming in here and ordering me around at the point of a pistol. I represent the United States government, you know. I'll have the sheriff on you for this.'

'Now that's not smart thinking. I can do this just because I do have the pistol. As for your being a government man, what will the Denver office say when I tell them you have been known not to send messages that folks paid to have sent? Now,' he brought the barrel down to point directly between the operator's eyes, 'start sending. Please.'

Mumbling to himself, the operator picked up the message and turned back to his equipment. Cordy and Caleb watched as the key clicked a steady stream. Completing the operation, the man turned back toward the counter.

'All right? Are you satisfied now?'

Cordy nodded and shoved his Colt back in the holster. 'Now you can sell me a ticket to Denver on today's train.'

Standing outside the waiting-room with the ticket in his hand, Cordy turned to Caleb.

'Here's a note to Mr Colfield suggesting that he hire you.' He looked the man over, dug deeper into his pocket and took out a few coins. 'And here, get yourself an outfit. You won't get any riding job looking like an out-of-work banker. You can pay me back later. You got a horse?'

'Yeah. I never got to the point I had to sell my horse and saddle. Came close a couple times but there was always the saloon to swamp out.'

'Funny that Bosewell would let you hang around.'

'Ah, I think he liked the idea of my reaching the bottom with no place to go. I was just as stubborn and wouldn't leave. By the way, do you really know the code those telegraph people use?'

'Nope, but he didn't know that. Fact is, I only know about cows and horses, a bit more about guns but when it comes to things like the telegraph I'm lost. Truth to tell, this will be the first time I've been on a train, too.'

Caleb laughed. 'I'll say this, you got nerve.'

'C'mon. I have to find a place for my horse while I'm gone.'

As they walked down to the livery stable

neither man noticed the skinny telegraph operator locking the door of the waiting-room and cutting over to the hotel.

CHAPTER SIX

'What do you mean, you sent a telegram to Denver about there being jobs at the Boxed C?' Marsh Bosewell snarled. 'I thought I made it clear there wasn't going to be any messages sent like that.' Anger turned his chubby cheeks red.

'Yes, sir, you did,' the other man whimpered. 'But this young man held his gun on me. He said he could read Morse code and if I didn't sent it now and send it right, he'd shoot me. I had to do what he said. You can see that, can't you?'

Bosewell, sitting at his desk in the second-floor office he used when in town, threw the pen he had been holding across the room. 'Damn it, man. I got that fool Colfield by the short hairs and I don't need to have no fool coming in now to upset things.'

He settled back in his chair and let his eyes take in the street outside, using the time to bring his temper under control.

'So, you sent his message. That means I'll have to do something about it. Anything else you got to say for yourself?'

'No, sir. He paid for the telegram and a round trip ticket to Denver. There wasn't anything I could do about it except come let you know.'

'He's going to Denver? On today's train?' Bosewell's eyes thinned as he thought about that. Then he came to a decision. He glanced back at the skinny man. 'Get out of here. I'll take care of your mistake. And send Blanchard and that idiot he hangs around with up as you go out.'

Ike Blanchard and his partner, Morton Olivera, thought they had stumbled onto a good thing when hiring on at the B-Bar-B. The two men had met in Denver and hearing that there was work for hard men handy with a gun they caught the next train to Silver Canyon. Neither especially liked the looks of their new boss or the man Price, but they took the job, liking the money. So far the work had been light and the money good.

'Get in here,' Bosewell snarled when one of the two big men knocked on the office door. 'I've got a job for you.'

Cordy was uncomfortable, sitting on the hard leather seat midway down the narrow rail car. He felt his stomach jump when the engine, after sounding its whistle to tell the world it was departing, lurched into motion with a jerk. Grabbing onto the arm of the seat in near panic, he held his body rigid and peered with eyes wide open as the train picked up speed. Only as he became accustomed to the rolling and shaking was he able to relax. Even then, watching the sagebrush whip past his window made his back muscles stiffen, especially when the car passed through a cut, the rocky soil looking to be only inches from the fast-moving train. The next time, he swore silently, he'd go by horseback.

As the sun dropped behind a range of tall mountains and dusk came on, a portly uniformed man came through the car lighting kerosene lanterns. Cordy had been paying so much attention to the world passing by outside that he hadn't noticed anything else. Now with the soft glow of the lanterns lighting the interior he took in the rest of the car.

Ahead near the door at the front of the car he saw the backs of a man and woman. When the woman bent forward and picked up a child to hold against her shoulder, he decided it would be a family. They looked to be relaxed and he figured they must have been used to riding the train. Behind them a few seats and on the other side of the car, a man he took to be a salesman sat with his hat pulled down over his eyes, asleep.

Not wanting to get caught staring at

anyone, he leaned forward, glancing behind him before settling back on the hard seat. Two men, sitting with their hats pulled low over their faces had taken seats on each side of the corridor that ran down the center of the car.

He hadn't asked how late the train would get into Denver but, after pulling his own dusty Stetson down, he leaned his head back thinking it'd be good if he could catch up on his sleep. Unable totally to relax, he was about ready to give up when he felt something jab him in the back.

'Now, mister, this here's a Colt poking in your ribs. Do what we tell you and you'll come out of here in one piece. Cause any trouble and I'll simply drop the hammer. Don't make any mind to me either way, but any shooting and that family up there is likely to get hurt.'

'What're you doing? Robbing a passenger? Tell you the truth, I ain't got but a few dollars in my pocket.'

The man behind him chuckled. 'No, it ain't your measly few coins we want. Listen to me, there's two of us so don't do anything foolish. You paying attention?'

'So far I'm hearing you.'

'Good. Now we want you to stand up, slow and easy like. Keep both your hands a long way from that Colt you're wearing while you do it.'

Hesitating until he was jabbed in the back again, Cordy stood up and waited.

The man chuckled again. 'Now that's right smart of you. Keep it slow and easy. Turn and follow my partner keeping your hands out where I can see them. Go on, move it.'

Cordy glanced across the aisle at the second man sitting with his revolver pointing up at him. When that man stood and moved ahead, he dropped in behind, keeping his hands in plain view. Trying to think of how he was going to get out of the trouble he was in, he followed, being pushed by the gun barrel pressed in the small of his back.

Staying a few steps behind the man in front, he wasn't prepared when that fellow stepped through the door out onto a platform over the swaying coupling between the cars. He looked down at the ground rushing by and forgot about the gunmen in his panic. He was about to step back into the safety of the car when the man behind him brought his gun barrel down on Cordy's head. A flash of pain disappearing into darkness was the last thing he felt as he fell.

CHAPTER SEVEN

Sunlight burning through his closed eyelids made him move his head, a shift that brought a groan as a giant ache filled his cranium. The deep throbbing pain seemed to ease only when darkness moved in as he passed back into the soft quiet of unconsciousness.

The next time the heat of the sun hit his upturned face all he could do was turn his head, stopping only when the world started spinning. Gasping he opened his eyes in near panic.

After a long minute of looking up at the blue sky, afraid of making any sudden movement, he reached up to feel his pounding head. He sat up, leaned over and closed his eyes as he tried to remember where he was. The last thing he could recall was sitting on something hard, trying to get comfortable. The worn black leather seat in that passenger car on the train. Then in a sudden rush he remembered the two men.

He jerked his eyes open and looked around. The men and the train were gone. His hat, lying a few feet way, caught his eye. He pulled it on, being careful not to put any pressure on the back of his skull. Having the bright sun blocked from his eyes helped and he was able to turn his head without causing the hammering between his eyes to intensify.

What he saw didn't make him feel any better. The sun was just clearing the top of a cut in the hillside, making the twin steel rails running up the track and coming together in the distance sparkle. They had knocked him out and tossed him off the train.

He dropped a hand to his side and felt emptiness; they had taken his gunbelt. When he tried to get to his feet he saw they had stripped his boots off, too.

'Damn,' he croaked, his throat suddenly feeling dry and cracked. Kneeling, he brushed off his hands and swore silently. Those boots were almost brand new and were just starting to feel good. More important, without them he wouldn't be walking very far.

'No gun, no boots and no water. A helluva fix to be in, Mister. A hell of a fix.' And, he added silently, already talking to myself.

Alright, what are you going to do, give up? What was it Zeb had said time after time? A man can always figure something out if he sets his mind to it. Or was it something that Cletus had tried to teach him. So, think.

He had been taking the train into Denver to see a man about hiring a crew. The plan had been to return by the morning train. That meant there'd be a train coming sometime. And that meant he'd have to be ready for it. Denver, he remembered, was south and east of Silver Canyon so the train, when it came, would be heading that way. Now, how does one stop a train in the middle of nowhere?

As he looked around all he could see was dirt and a few straggly bushes. Not enough to stop a squirrel.

Well, if the train was coming and the engineer was watchful, anything on the track might make him slow down. If it looked big enough, it might even make him stop.

Not knowing how long he had he got to work, and ignoring the pain in his head and the tenderness of his feet, he started pulling at all the brush he could jerk free, piling it up to make it look big. All the time he kept a watch on the track, wanting to be ready when the train eventually came.

He sat down against the far side of the cut through the hill, in as much shade as he could find. He tried to ignore his headache and not think about being thirsty. Slowly the sun moved higher in the morning sky. He kept his head bowed and tried to urge the ball of fire to move faster.

The sun was high in the sky when he heard the rails start to hum. He looked down the track but couldn't see any change. The pile of brush, held down with a few bigger rocks from blowing in the little breeze that had sprung up, didn't look big enough but it was all he could do. Climbing around, pulling and breaking off limbs from the sun-dried bushes, he'd cut his feet in a couple places. Eventually he had given up. It was either enough or . . . he didn't finish that thought; it'd have to be enough.

His brush pile turned out to be enough; he heard the long whistle and figured that that was when the engineer saw something on the track ahead. The sound of the engine slowing came right after. Cordy waited until the engine had pulled level with him before standing up.

'Hey, Buck,' someone called out, 'watch out, there's a jasper over there in the shade.'

'Don't move, mister,' another voice called. 'We got us a couple rifles here.'

Cordy, with both hands held high, stepped into the morning sunlight.

'All right by me. I'm not any kind of bad hold-up man. I've got a return trip ticket here in my pocket, Denver to Silver Canyon. If you don't mind, I'd like to take advantage of it.'

'What? What do ya mean,' said a man wearing an oily-looking black-and-gray striped billed cap who stood in the engine's open doorway, 'you got a ticket? Does this look like a train station?'

'Nope. Don't really look like a good place to stop, but it's the best I could do. Mind if I climb aboard? I can explain better if I was up there sitting down and enjoying a drink of water. It's been a while.'

'Well,' the cap wearing man hesitated, 'I dunno.'

'Buck, you know the company rule about anyone riding in the cab.'

'Ah, hell, Henry, of course I do. Can't just let this feller stand there in the hot sun, though, can we? No, sir, we can't,' he answered himself. 'Come on, stranger. Climb on up here. Buck, see his feet? He ain't in no shape to be clearing off the track. You climb down and kick it outa the way. There isn't as much there as it looked there was. Go on, now, move it. We're gonna be behind schedule as it is.'

'OK, mister,' said Buck once everybody was back on board and the engine was again speeding across the flat land. 'Mind telling us how you come to be out there? And what's that about having a return ticket?'

Cordy pulled it from his shirt pocket and handed it to the engineer before telling him about being attacked and thrown off the outgoing train.

'Now I'll have to report this to the sheriff when we pull into Silver Canyon.'

Cordy thought about it a moment, then frowned. 'I'd appreciate it if you just forgot all about picking me up. I got an idea it'd be better for me if whoever didn't want me to get to Denver didn't know I was back in town.'

'What kind of devilment are you up to that someone would want to stop you from going to Denver?'

'Tell you the truth, I'm not all that sure. It seems to be trouble between a greedy cattleman and all the smaller ranchers in the basin.'

'Uh huh, I've heard something about that. For some time only one ranch has been doing any shipping. Horses and cattle, all with the same brand. Well, bucking the big boys can be dangerous. But from the looks of you, I ain't telling you anything you don't know.'

Cordy chuckled softly. 'I had a friend a while back who said something about talking softly and striking hard and fast. Maybe all the danger won't go on being one-sided.'

When they reached town Cordy waited until the engine had come to a stop before climbing gingerly down from the cab. He tossed a wave back at the men looking down at him, and, keeping out of sight of the waiting room, carefully made his way toward the other end of town. It took time, staying out of sight by slowly walking in the brush behind all the buildings that faced onto Main Street. When he reached the back of the livery, he stopped just inside the wide back doors and let his eyes adjust to the cool gloom.

He waited until he saw the stable owner leave the tack room to take care of a rider's horse, then he crept from stall to stall until he could slip into the little room. It was the work of a minute to dig his saddlebags out of the pile and get back out of sight in an empty stall.

First he took out his pa's holstered Starr revolver and buckled it around his waist. Then he dug deeper to remove the sack of gold he had hidden rolled up in a dirty shirt. Keeping a sharp lookout, he was able to return the leather saddlebags to the tack room before stepping out into the noontime sunshine. Feeling better with the gun on his hip, he thought it was time to see about a new pair of boots. And maybe a new shirt, too, before he went hunting.

CHAPTER EIGHT

Harold Peeves watched as Cordy strode through his store, walking gingerly on his bare feet, heading toward the back wall where the supply of high-heeled boots was shelved. Nothing was said until the young cowhand eventually found a pair he liked. He picked up a shirt and a new Stetson and he laid his purchases out on the counter.

'I hope you got enough money to pay for that stuff, young man. Those boots don't come cheap.'

'It's my habit to pay for what I need. And to collect what's owed me, too,' Cordy responded, dropping his little sack of gold on the counter. 'I reckon there'll be enough here to pay what I owe so I can get on with my business.'

Peeves untied the poke's drawstrings and looked inside. Then he nodded and reached under the counter for a small set of balance scales. 'Not often we get raw gold any more. There was a time, but, well, I guess all the gold that's to be found has been picked up. Where'd it all come from?'

Cordy chuckled. 'You don't have to worry about it, all you have to do is weigh it. And don't worry none about wrapping up the boots or the hat. I'll be wearing them.'

Peeves, smile barely lifted his lips as he tied a string around the bundle containing the shirt while Cordy stomped on the new boots.

'I have to admit, I like doing business with you. Bring your gold in any time,' Peeves said.

Cordy nodded, made sure his new hat was comfortably settled on his still aching head, took his package and left the store. He stopped on the boardwalk and thought about what he was going to do. He had drunk almost all the water the engineer had been carrying but he hadn't had anything to eat, not since before getting on the train. A meal and a few hours' sleep and he thought he'd be ready for anything.

The sun was well above the horizon the next morning when, after a hearty breakfast he walked out of the restaurant to stand for a moment to map out his next move. Before dropping off to sleep the day before he had thought about what had happened. The only people in town who had known of his plans had been that cowboy he'd sent out to the ranch and the ticket agent. That would be the same ticket agent who had somehow 'lost' Miss Colfield's telegram to her hiring contact in Denver. That would be a good place to ask questions, he figured.

Feeling rested and wearing his new shirt, he started walking down the street only to stop. Coming up the boardwalk toward him were three men, two of them he recognized. He thumbed the thong off the hammer of the Starr and waited.

'Now will you look who's here,' he called out when the men were about twenty feet from him. 'Last time we met was on the train.'

The men stopped and looked up to see who it was. 'Well, well, Mort, look what we have here,' one of the men snarled. 'How in hell did you get back to town?'

'Oh, it wasn't all that hard. I've been thinking about you two.' Without taking his eyes off the pair, Cordy noticed that the third man had disappeared. 'You there, what's that I see around your gut? Looks like my gunbelt. Gentlemen,' Cordy said, letting a cold smile build, 'you can make it easy by just dropping my gunbelt on the ground and walking away. Or you can make your play.'

'You're crazy. Must have rattled your brain pan when we tossed you off the train.' One of the men laughed and dropped his hand to the revolver hanging low on his hip. 'You got any idea what's gonna happen to you? Bracing Mort and me ain't the smartest thing you've ever done. Why, I've killed my share of men. You won't be the first. I'm Ike Blanchard, maybe you've heard of me?'

Cordy laughed and shook his head. 'Nope.

Likely wouldn't remember anyhow. Never did have time for gossip about would-be bad men. Save yourself some trouble. Just drop my gunbelt.'

Blanchard snorted, 'Hell, I've had enough of this.' He drew his pistol.

At his move, Cordy pulled his pa's Starr and shot the gunslinger before his gun had cleared leather. Mort was a bit slower but got his shot off, the slug hitting the post next to Cordy. Taking his time, Cordy drove his bullet squarely in the center of the man's chest. The three shots sounded to Sheriff Dallas, who had been crossing the street at the time, almost like one.

'Hey,' Dallas yelled as he came up on the boardwalk, 'that'll be enough of that.'

Replacing the empties in the Starr, Cordy nodded. 'Yeah, I guess you're right.'

Stepping over, he unbuckled the gunbelt holding his Colt from around Mort's body. Hanging it over a shoulder he looked at the Sheriff. 'You have a problem with any of this?'

'Well, we don't like any shooting in town.

But from what I saw and heard, I reckon these two asked for it. Not too bright on your part, though, coming up against two hardcases.'

'I had a good teacher. He told me never to back down but to make every shot count. Now, if it's all right with you, I think it's time I headed back out to the ranch.'

No-nose John had worked for the Bosewells since he was a youngster. His first memories were of the US Army post outside which his pa and ma had set up their teepee. Little Coyote, as his mother called him, grew up eating the meat and grain his pa begged from the soldiers' cook. If he couldn't beg enough he stole what was needed. It was only natural that, when reaching his tenth summer, the boy stole a horse from the post's herd.

The horse was a big-boned Army mount, a lot bigger animal than the little ponies the Indians hanging around the fort had. Little Coyote simply climbed onto the horse's back and rode away. When the sour-smelling sergeant caught the boy, he pulled the youngster off the horse, backhanding him, knocking him head over heels. Without a backward glance the soldier simply rode back to the fort leaving the boy unconscious in the dirt.

When he came awake Little Coyote found he could only breathe through his mouth. The sergeant's blow had battered his nose flat. It was the white man, Price, who had given him the name No-nose John. For a long time Little Coyote didn't understand what the man was telling him but he understood that the big man had saved him. From that day on, he followed the big man and did whatever he was directed to do, being ordered by growls and finger-pointing. Then one day, as if by magic, the gruff words began to make sense. He knew he owed it all to the man, Price, and if the man wanted to call him No-nose John, that was alright.

It had been Price who had shown him what to do, how to shoot a rifle and how to work around the ranch. One of the jobs he was given as a youngster was to keep the branding fires burning at round-up time. When Price and his men caught a couple rustlers, No-nose had been along.

'Well,' Price had said, looking at the two men lying on the ground, 'if there's one thing I can't abide, it's a rustler. Going around stealing another man's livestock is the worse thing someone can do. Now we're going to teach you not to steal no more. No-nose, light up one of your hot little fires.'

The hands sat around and rolled their smokes, waiting to see what Price was going to do. When the fire burned down to a bed of fiery embers, Price took a ranch branding-iron from his saddlebag and tossed it to the Indian.

'There you go, boy. Heat this up.'

'What are you gonna do?' one of the rustlers cried.

'Teach you a lesson, son. Just teach you a lesson.'

Neither of the rustlers lived through the pain of being branded, but No-nose came away from where they left the bodies a happy man. Price had tossed him a rifle that one of the dead men had been carrying. He'd never owned such a good thing before.

Being one of the B-Bar-B's crew meant that nobody gave him a second look when he walked down the dirt streets of the town. Walking down the street made No-nose proud, even though he didn't think much of the two men he had been walking with that morning. When a stranger called out to the two men, No-nose saw there was trouble coming.

Quickly he stepped aside, ducked down an alley and got away. After hearing the gunshots, he figured he'd better tell Bosewell what had happened. The two men, after all, had worked for Bosewell.

CHAPTER NINE

'What?' Bosewell snarled after No-nose finished telling him of the shooting. 'Describe the stranger.'

'Him young, has hair the color of dried grass. Was wearing new hat and boots with no dust on them.'

'Hmm, I wonder. Only one man would have a problem with Blanchard or that partner of his. Alright, No-nose, you did good, coming to tell me. Now I want you to ride out to the ranch and tell Price to come in. You understand?'

'Huh.' The Indian nodded and left without another word.

'New hat and boots, huh,' Bosewell said to

himself. 'Wonder if Peeves knows anything about that fellow? Or maybe the sheriff?'

He grabbed his hat and stomped down the stairs and out onto the street.

'Good morning, Mr Bosewell,' Peeves greeted him.

Bosewell liked the fact that everyone in town called him mister. Just as it should be, he thought; these fools wouldn't last a month without him and his ranch. They knew it'd be a lot better for them when the entire basin carried the B-Bar-B brand.

'Two of my men were shot a while ago by a young man wearing a new hat and boots. You make a sale like that recently?'

'Well, yes I did. Said he was working for old man Colfield. Was in here a day or so ago, too. Told me'n the sheriff that he was going to try to hire some hands. Yes, I sold him a pair of boots, a shirt and a new Stetson. Paid with raw gold, he did. Nice batch of nuggets and dust. First gold I've seen in a long time.'

Bosewell, his mind on his thoughts almost missed the word gold. It wasn't what he was expecting at all. 'Wait a minute . . . gold, you say?'

'Yep. Had a little poke about half-filled with the lovely stuff.'

'Hmm, well, that's interesting. Say where he got it?'

Peeves chuckled. 'Nope. Not likely around here, though. I haven't heard of anyone fording any little pockets in a long time.'

Bosewell nodded. 'Hmm, all right. You told me what I expected. Thanks.'

As he walked back down the street to his office the rancher was thinking, hoping that that damn Indian came back in with Price. He had another job for him to take care of.

Price, followed by the Indian, came into Bosewell's office and threw himself into one of the wooden chairs, putting his shabby worn boots on a corner of the desk and leaning back. No-nose John simply folded his arms across his chest and leaned against the closed door.

'Wal, boss. What you got in mind fer me?'

'In a minute. No-nose, you remember that

youngster that shot up Blanchard and his partner?'

The Indian didn't speak but nodded his head once.

'Yeah, I thought you would. Well it seems he bought some stuff over at Peeves's store and paid for it with raw gold. Now what I want you to do is go find out where that yellow metal come from. Make him tell you, I don't care much how you do it, but make him tell you before you kill him. Should be easy, he's young and likely careless. It should be easy for you but make damn sure you find out before you kill him. You understand me?'

The Indian nodded once more and left the room.

'What's that, boss? You saying Ike got hisself killed? Well, it don't surprise me none. Both he and that big fella he's been running with didn't exactly stand out.'

'Price, few of those gunnies you hired are worth their salt. As soon as I get what I want outa this basin I want them all gone. One thing I don't need is a bunch of hardcases eating me outa house and home.'

'Yeah, there ain't none of them what'll hang around if the payday money is cut off.'

'Yeah, well, that's likely. But we're not through with them yet. The kid that shot Blanchard and the other jasper has gone to work for Colfield out at the Boxed C. Old Zach Colfield is proving to be stubborn. I want you to send some of those gunnies out there to harass him some. Don't kill him, but make his life a mite uncomfortable. I want him to be thinking about selling out to me. He's got that good-looking daughter of his and I don't want anything to happen to her either. The folks around here like the money you and the boys spend but if anything was to happen to her, they'd turn on us quicker than a rattlesnake strikes.'

Price chuckled. 'Wal, I can't say I wouldn't like to get nice and cozy with that little filly but you're right. There's other ways to make old man Colfield want to look for a quieter life somewheres else.'

'All right, just see that it's done.'

CHAPTER TEN

Cordy didn't know exactly what to say. He'd gone into town thinking he'd at least find a few hands to bring out to the Boxed C but came back almost empty-handed. Caleb had turned up and handed the note to Zach Colfield who read it, talked to the cowboy a little and hired him.

'Hannah said she'd seen him around town a few times and didn't know he was a rider,' he said when Cordy asked. 'Carl knew about him and kinda stood up for him. Said he remembered him when he rode for the Lazy R. Anyway, I figured it couldn't hurt. Leastways as long as I can afford to make a payroll.'

As he stood on the veranda, looking down at the wheelchair-bound man, Cordy regarded his own long fingers working the brim of his hat. 'Boss, I don't know what to say. I really thought there'd be at least a few men in town willing to work but that Bosewell's got his scare in. The sheriff laid it out for me and I can't really blame him or the others in town but, darn it, it didn't go like I thought it would.'

He hadn't mentioned his short train ride or getting thrown off the train.

'Mr Lowell,' Hannah cut in, 'don't feel bad about it. We've been getting used to seeing the way things have gone around here. You said you did get the telegram sent, didn't you?' Cordy glanced at the girl and nodded. 'Well, maybe something good will come of that.'

He almost smiled, hearing her try to make him feel better. Somehow he liked it.

'Maybe,' said Zach Colfield, letting his gaze search out into the distance. 'But it'd have to happen pretty quick. That bank note is due in another month or so and I think that's all Bosewell's waiting for.'

Cordy frowned and thought about the little bag of gold he had in his saddlebags. There was enough there to keep him fed for a while but not a lot more. Certainly not enough to meet any bank note.

'Well, meanwhile I guess the three of us, Carl, Caleb and me, can go see what we can do about fixing that fence and pushing back the Lazy R beef.'

Colfield didn't comment but nodded before turning to wheel himself into the house.

'Mr Lowell,' Hannah started to say when Cordy interrupted her, holding up a hand.

'Miss Hannah, it'd be a lot better if you dropped the mister and just called me Cordy. I'd feel better about it.'

The young woman smiled and nodded. 'All right, if you'll drop the "Miss". It does seem formal and not like we're going to work together.'

'Tell me a little about that bank note. It isn't

any of my business, but. . . .'

'Oh well, I don't know exactly. All I know is the note is due in just over a month and I know Father doesn't have enough to pay it off. He was working on the books again last night and I heard him mumbling to himself. The price of beef at the railhead is pretty good right now and he thinks if we could get even a hundred head to market we could pay the note.'

'Miss Hannah, uh, Hannah, there might be another way. I'd have to make a trip north but . . . well, I don't really want to have to say anything else but . . . I think it's worth a try. The three of us going out and working on the fence won't make any difference, not to meeting that bank note. There is just no way we could round up enough stock, even if we could get a herd past Bosewell and his men. I . . . well, I think there might be another way.'

'What ever you're thinking about, it isn't, well, illegal, is it?'

'No, it's nothing like that. It's just . . . well, it's kinda hard to explain. A couple old men trusted me with a secret and . . . well, I guess that's all.'

Hannah looked down at her hands. 'It's just that we don't know much about you. I didn't think you were dishonest, but. . . .' She let the thought fade away.

Cordy nodded. 'That's all right. No harm done. My horse has had a couple days' rest and the ride will do him good. I figure it'll take two, maybe three weeks.'

'Will you take Caleb or Carl with you?'

'No, it's best if I ride alone. I'd keep them working close, though. Your pa doesn't think Bosewell will do anything until the note comes due so you should be alright but it wouldn't hurt to have a couple extra guns around the place just in case. You just never know.'

The sun hadn't risen above the mountain range to the east when Cordy rode out the next morning. Hannah had breakfast ready for him and it was still dark when the three hands joined her and her father in the kitchen for eggs, bacon, hash browns and thick-sliced toast. After asking Carl and Caleb to keep a sharp eye out he saddled his chestnut gelding and headed north.

The high country where Zeb and Cletus had made their home, and where Cordy had healed, was a couple days' ride north of the little town of Durango. After Zeb had died and Cletus decided to go south to spend his remaining days in the sunshine along river country, down on the Texas-Mexican border, it had been in Durango that they had split up. Cletus sitting comfortably on the leather seats of a stagecoach and Cordy on horseback, starting his search for a certain man and a particular horse.

It had taken him almost three years to find his way from Durango south to Silver Canyon, working here and there along the way. Years he'd spent growing into the man he now was. Now, after setting a steady pace he was riding down the dirt street of Durango just two weeks after leaving the Boxed C.

He left his gelding at the stable, chomping at a bait of oats with a promise of a good rub-down to follow, and took time for a bath in one of the tubs behind the Chinaman's laundry. Careful to keep his brand-scarred chest hidden, he let the hot water soothe his saddle-weary muscles. Not wanting to waste any time, he decided it wouldn't hurt to spend one night sleeping on one of the hotel's soft mattresses.

The next morning he felt like a new man. He wasn't sure whether it was the bath, a good night's sleep or wearing clothes that the Chinaman had washed all the road dirt out of. He didn't give it another thought and was on the trail north after a final cup of coffee at the little Mexican restaurant next to the hotel.

As he rode out of town, heading back to the little valley with its hidden cabin, Cordy wondered what shape he'd find it in. Possibly it was thinking of those days of riding with Zeb and Cletus after making one of their trips into town that made him aware he was being followed.

The two old-timers had been very careful not to lead anyone back to their favorite country and, without thinking much about it, Cordy had been following the same habits. The second day out of Durango, while topping a windswept ridge just above the tree line, high in the rugged mountain range, he doubled back and, carrying his Henry, chose a little sheltered pocket in the rocks and settled in for a rest. His horse had been left hobbled in a small meadow on the other side from where he sat in the deep shade of two huge boulders. He called the Henry rifle his, but it had once been Zeb's and for a long time he thought of it as being the old man's gun.

The sun was about an hour from dropping behind the higher mountains behind him when he caught a flash of movement below where he sat, his back against one of the boulders. Careful not to move he watched as a man, sitting slumped in his saddle, his head down, came up out of the darkness of the forest behind him. The rider was tracking him.

From where he was sat the tracker was too far away for Cordy to make out much about him. Cordy swore silently when he realized that if the stranger stayed on the trail left by his gelding he wouldn't come much closer either. At the same time he realized his predicament; he couldn't very well let this stranger find his hobbled horse.

Cordy moved as soon as the stranger disappeared, heading back as fast as he could to the little meadow. When he had gone off to start his backtracking, he had reined to the left, following a faint game trail along the brush-covered upper edge of the slope. If the tracker was any good he couldn't miss seeing where Cordy had turned off. Maybe he should stop just above where his horse was hobbled and set up an ambush. That, he decided when he found a likely place, would be something that Cletus would have done.

He settled himself, carefully levered a shell into the breech of the rifle and, making sure he had a good field of fire, waited.

CHAPTER ELEVEN

The heat of the day faded fast after the sun dropped out of sight behind the far mountains. Cordy sat with his elbows on his knees, ready to move his sight at the first sign of the man following him. For a long few minutes he waited and the man didn't show up.

How long should he wait? Dusk was coming on and it would make hitting a moving target harder. Thinking about it, Cordy made the decision to move. Most likely, when the tracker came to where the horse he was following had been reined off to backtrack, he'd stopped to consider. With the coming darkness the man would likely figure it would be dangerous to go much further. The trail would still be there the next morning.

Cordy scooted down to get his horse.

Careful now, he rode out of the meadow, cutting back toward the game trail. Dark came quickly as he dropped down the ridge. Before it got too dark, he knew he'd have to find a place to hole up for the night, somewhere where he could be protected and a place he could get out of at first light.

At some time in the past, a huge pine tree had fallen, leaving a large swale in the soft earth where the tree's root system had pulled free. There was enough light in the dusk for Cordy to see that there was room enough for both his horse and himself. He wouldn't build a fire and would have a cold camp.

Lying in his bedroll, before falling asleep, he tried to come up with a plan for taking care of whoever was behind him. Nothing came to mind as his eyes closed.

Up before the sun, Cordy rode up and over the next ridge and the one after that, always climbing higher into the mountains. Early in the afternoon, three days after discovering he was being followed, he reached familiar country. He and Caleb had hunted deer in the little valley below.

At some time in the distant past fire had swept through this part of the forest, leaving behind a treeless slope. Wild grasses, growing tall and covering the hillside gave deer and other animals both food and cover. Caleb had shown the youngster how, after leaving their mules tied securely just above the edge of the forest, to creep stealthily down to the wide, shallow creek that wandered along the bottom. Thick clumps of willows growing on either creek bank were a favorite place for deer to sleep through the heat of the day.

Sitting his saddle, looking down, he thought about the man he'd spotted tracking him. There had been no sign of the tracker since that first sighting. Could it have been that there was no tracker? In all the time he'd spent up in these mountains with Caleb and Zeb they hadn't run into another person. But not having seen anyone or any sign of his being followed made Cordy wonder. Had there actually been someone on his trail back there? Looking down at the tall grass he thought this might be a good place to find out.

He lifted the reins of the gelding and started down through the tall grass, leaving a wide trail behind him. He broke through the screening willows and reined the horse upstream keeping in the middle of the water course. After about a mile he kneed the horse out of the creek and into a small clearing. He hobbled his mount, took the rifle and set off back through the trees to the open area. On finding a suitable place, where he had a clear view of the little valley, he settled once again to wait, this time behind a large pine log. From where he sat the trail he'd left through the grass was within rifle range.

Chewing on a piece of dried beef and keeping an eye on the hillside, he gave his situation more thought. Somehow he'd have to get rid of the tracker before heading to the log cabin and then on up to the pool. He didn't have a long time to accomplish this.

Hannah had said the loan to the bank would come due in about a month. He'd been on the trail now for about half that. He didn't have a lot of time to waste on this tracker.

Thinking about Hannah, he let his mind focus on how he felt when talking with her. She was the first girl of his own age he'd ever talked to. A time or two, back when going into Durango with Zeb and Caleb, they had spent some time talking with the woman who owned the general store and he remembered how much he'd liked that. It was different, standing next to Hannah Colfield and talking with her. Somehow he felt like there were just the two of them when that happened. Nothing else and no one else mattered.

Thoughts of Hannah fled when he caught movement in the grass above the trail he'd left. A soft breeze had been blowing, bending the seed pods along the tops of the grass stems in one direction. The movement he saw was forcing the tops another way. Bringing the Henry's front sights around, he squinted along the barrel and waited. For a long few minutes nothing moved; the grass was still. Then he saw how the grass in the place he was watching started moving, just like all the grass around it. The tracker was gone.

As quickly as possible, and keeping out of sight of the grass-covered slope, Cordy scurried back to where he'd hobbled his horse. The gelding was calmly chopping at the few clumps of grass growing in the clearing.

'Dumb animal,' Cordy cursed to himself. 'Not smart enough to know we're in trouble.'

He mounted up and headed on up the valley, making his own trail through the thickening forest. Figuring he'd wasted the best part of half a day on the failed ambush, he now headed more directly toward the hidden valley and the log cabin. Somewhere, somehow, he'd have to come up with a better plan.

Things appeared to be about the same when he caught sight of the small wide valley. He had expected things to have changed in the years since he and Caleb had ridden out but from what he could tell everything was the same.

Riding down to the front of the log structure he saw how the grass growing in the sod on the roof was green and lush-looking. The door was still closed tightly, just as they'd left it.

'Got to give those two old boys a lot of credit,' he said as he unsaddled the gelding and gave the animal a good rub down. 'They built this place to last and it's sure doing it.'

Inside there were a few signs that some small animals had taken up residence, half-chewed seeds were scattered on the plank flooring and a couple holes had been gnawed in some sacking left behind. At some point wind blowing down the rock wall at the back had blown a thin covering of ashes out of the simple rock fireplace and onto the floor. Mice tracks crossed that gray dusting, reminding him of the tracker who had followed the track left by his horse.

'I wonder what that fella will think when he comes along my trail and spots the cabin?

Now,' he mused aloud, 'if it were me, I'd see the front of the place and if there was a horse left in the shelter over there, I'd think someone was home. Maybe the person I was following, thinking he was safe and secure. So then wouldn't I just sneak up on the cabin and. . .?'

Nodding Cordy took up his Henry, closed the door behind him and cut out through the trees. 'Time for another ambush,' he muttered to himself.

The rest of that afternoon he sat with his back against a tree, his trail-dusty clothes blending in so that he was almost invisible. He waited. Birds flitted through the trees, singing down along the creek and generally went about their business. A little after the sun went down but before it got too dark to see, a handful of does came slowly, watchfully up away from the creek to start feeding. Sitting and not moving Cordy watched the deer until, feeling safe, a big buck strolled out of the willows and lowered his horn-heavy head to pull at the grass.

There was no sign of the tracker.

After darkness had settled in, Cordy circled around, keeping to the trees, back down to the cabin and lit a fire in the stone fireplace to cook his meal. Savoring his coffee he decided not to put it off: the next morning he'd head up to the pool. There wasn't enough time left to waste on trying to trap the tracker. Somehow he'd have to deal with that another way. He spent that night, as he'd spent all the others since seeing the tracker, without a fire, wrapped in his blankets hidden back in the trees.

'Face it, there hasn't been any sign of that fella following me since back on that slope. Not really. I could be getting the jimjams, afraid of my own shadow.'

In addition, he thought, time was running out for him. Say he gave two days at bringing up gravel from the bottom of the pool and panning out what gold there was. And then a rush back to Silver Canyon to the bank. That might be cutting it close, but he should be in time.

Back in the trees and rolled in his blankets, with his rifle lying close to his hand, Cordy fell asleep. He didn't see the shadow move stealthily through the trees on the other side of the valley to come up to the cabin, stopping to gently pat the sleeping gelding on the rump. Edging around the cabin's corner the Indian pushed against the closed door, letting it inch open. Staying low, No-nose John crept far enough into the single room and froze in the darkness. Turning his head first one way and then the other he listened. Not hearing any sound, not even that of a sleeping man, he crawled back and disappeared in the night.

CHAPTER TWELVE

Up with the sun again the next morning Cordy fixed his breakfast in the fireplace before saddling his horse and riding out. He had noticed the cabin door not being as he left it but there hadn't been any other sign that someone had been there. To be safe he decided to believe he was still being followed and would take what precautions he could without wasting any more time. He'd be ready, he thought, and once he had enough gold he'd be damn hard to catch up with.

Although each time the two older men had taken him to the pool they had gone a slightly different way, Cordy didn't have any trouble finding the narrow canyon. Not wanting to fritter away much of the day, he still took the opportunity to back-track a couple times, not so much as to discover where the tracker was but more to cause the tracker to slow down. Maybe even to lose any trail the gelding was leaving behind.

Long before the two old men had found the injured young man, they had discovered the pool at the bottom of a rushing waterfall. While they were camping near the cold clear pool at the bottom of the rushing water, one of them had spotted a little bit of color mixed in the gravel creek bed. It didn't take them long to figure out that the sand and gravel at the bottom of the pool would likely hold more of the yellow metal.

Over the years of living in their hidden valley, they took out only as much gold as they needed. Trading the gold for supplies, flour, coffee, salt and the like, at the general store in Durango, they had been careful not to lead anyone to their treasure. Cordy had been the first and only person they had trusted with their find.

It was late afternoon when he came to the edge of the narrow canyon. The chestnut gelding didn't like the idea of going down the slip of a trail but at Cordy's urging it stepped tentatively on it. For the rider it was the same each and every time, the feeling of riding into emptiness. Part of his anxiety, he reasoned, trying to make himself feel safer, was caused by the thin narrow trail down the rocky face, but the loud, drumming of the falls down below was a big part of it.

Close to the bottom the noise from the waterfall was almost deafening, echoing within the constricted walls of the gorge. Riding out eventually on the bottom, he pulled up and looked back. Anyone following his hoofprints would easily see where he had gone over the upper lip, but once on the trail there would be no turning back.

'If I were sitting over there,' he glanced toward the rushing water, 'anyone coming down might not see me. Not if he was as anxious as I was the first time.' Or, he added silently, every time.

Poking a heel in the gelding's flank, he rode on up to the little flat ground next to the pool and stripped the saddle from his horse. Everything was just as he and Caleb had left it the last time they had been there. After Zeb had died and the two had come up with their own plans, they had made one last trip to the pool, each coming away with a small soft leather sack filled with nuggets and dust. As always, mist from the waterfall floated in the air, masking the other side of the small lake.

After putting the hobbles on the horse and covering his saddle gear with the groundcloth from his bedroll, he took his rifle and went back down the creek.

Away from the waterfall, the mist was much lighter and he took the time to carefully wipe his weapon down with his neckerchief. With the thin line of the trail in full view and using a large boulder to hide behind, he laid the Henry down and once again set himself to wait.

'Seems that's mostly what I've been doing,

setting up failed ambushes,' he muttered.

This time, though, had to be the last time. There was no place else to go.

Dusk came quickly as the sun moved westward, deepening the shadows in the bottom of the ravine. Any work on the gravel at the bottom of the pool would have to wait until morning.

He was thinking of the next day's effort when a small rock, falling from above and bouncing down the trail, caught his attention. Someone was coming down.

Checking to make sure there was a shell in the chamber, he waited, trying to breathe normally.

The horse looked small as it came carefully down the trail, the rider sitting on its back a shapeless bundle. Barely able to make out the form of the man, Cordy took careful aim at the bulky shape and fired.

The horse, feeling the man on its back fall, forgot where it was and jumped, hitting the bottom in a run. The bundle that he'd fired into bounced once before falling the last few feet onto the rocks at the bottom. Cordy, levering another shell into the chamber ran over to the body, keeping the barrel pointed and ready. The body didn't move.

Carefully, keeping a close watch in the failing light, Cordy used the rifle barrel to roll the body over, stopping when the wounded man groaned.

Seeing the long black braids, Cordy frowned, trying to remember where he'd seen the man before. Slowly, at first, then in a flash, it came back to him. It was the man who had put the red-hot branding iron to his chest.

'Damn you,' he yelled, pointing the Henry at the man's head and touching the trigger. He stopped when the Indian's eyes came open. 'Damn you to hell,' Cordy snarled.

But he didn't pull the trigger. Staring into the black centers of the man's eyes, Cordy felt like screaming.

'Do you know who I am?' he yelled, letting all his anger harden his words, his left hand brushing across the burning he felt in his chest.

The Indian didn't move. A foamy trickle of blood bubbled out of one corner of his mouth.

'Don't you die on me, damn you,' Cordy growled. 'Not until you recognize me. Remember? I'm the man you branded a few years back. Remember, damn you.'

The Indian lay motionless, only his eyes moving slowly from one side to the other as if looking for a way to escape, the foamy blood dribbling down his chin.

Cordy laughed coldly, almost insanely. 'What, you've set your brand on so many men you can't remember me? You and that fellow, Price. He stole my horse and you marked me. Ah, that got you. I saw your eyes. You do remember. You're going to die. Hell, you're already dead. That blood shows I got your lungs with my bullet. There is no way you're going to get out of here. It's too bad, though. I'd certainly like to put my mark on you like you did on me. Yeah. Mark you so when you get to your happy hunting ground everyone would know what kind of man you were.'

No-nose John might have understood, but there was no indication other than his eyes rolling back as he died.

The next day Cordy was busy, bringing bucket after bucket heavy with gravel from the bottom of the pool stopping only when he had to in order to catch his breath. All day he focused on his work. Not once did he think about the dead man back at the bottom of the trail. When darkness came on, he lit a fire and heated water for coffee and to cook his meal. A sound coming from behind made him jump, grabbing for his Colt. Standing with legs spread, the hammer of the revolver eared back, he had to laugh. It was the Indian's pony that he'd almost shot, a dusty gray mustang that looked either old or half-starved in the light of the small cook fire.

'So, you had enough of the dark, did you? Saw the fire and here you are. Well, you'll come in handy on the trip back, I expect.'

He stripped the worn and scarred saddle from the mustang, made up a set of hobbles and turned the animal off to feed in the same little grassy spot as his gelding.

Cordy looked over the pile of sand and rock he'd brought up from the bottom and knew that the next day, using a shallow pan to separate the gold out, would be another hard day.

CHAPTER THIRTEEN

It was difficult to tell whether he had enough gold; he didn't even know how much Colfield had borrowed for his fence. What he had in the saddlebags when he rode away from the pool would have to do.

Cordy had left behind the Indian's saddle and was leading the sorry-looking mustang by a long rope. Stopping to look down at the body, he thought for a minute about burying the man he'd killed.

'Nope, I guess not,' he said calmly. 'I'll just let the animals take care of your sorry carcass. You don't deserve the work it'd take to even cover you with rocks. C'mon, horse, let's get out of here.' He poked a heel in the gelding's flank and started up the trail.

When he stopped for the night at the cabin, Cordy looked the mustang over. After giving it some thought he decided not to trail it back.

'For sure someone would recognize you back in Silver Canyon,' he told the animal as he removed the halter from the horse's head. 'If'n you or that blamed Indian don't show up nobody'll ever know what happened.' He turned the animal loose and sent it on its way with a slap on the rump.

He watched as the mustang galloped a few yards away and then turned to look back, as if to question what to do next. 'It's quite likely that Bosewell put the Indian on my trail,' Cordy mused. 'Hard to say how he knew what I was up to, but I'll bet that's what happened. Well, let the big man wonder what happened. It'll do him good to be unsure and maybe worry about it.'

The next morning, after making sure his fire was completely out and the door firmly closed, he rode out of the little valley.

Looking back he wondered if he'd ever see it again. There had been no sign of the Indian's pony.

Even though he kept to the high country and stayed off any trail that might be used by anyone, the return trip to Silver Canyon only took three weeks of traveling. He was careful not to tire the gelding out but was able to maintain a steady pace. At one point Cordy had thought about stopping at the assayer's office in Durango, but didn't.

'Why let anyone know I've been up in the mountains? Carrying gold that no one knows I have is a lot safer than packing gold coin that others would see me with,' he explained to his horse. That decision allowed him to save a couple days' travel time too, he figured.

As he came to the little rise overlooking the Boxed C headquarters he stopped at just about the same spot he'd been when he first glimpsed the place. Cordy chuckled when he thought about that. That time he had sat and smoked a quirley but it had been more than a week since he'd run out of the makings. No more tobacco meant no smokes.

'Good thing we're back, horse.' He chuckled again, nudging the gelding down the little game trail. 'We're not only out of tobacco but the coffee sack is empty too.'

Cordy didn't see anyone when he rode slowly into the ranch yard and tied the reins to the rail in front of the main house. He stood to stretch his legs and he took a long look around. Everything looked about the same, but the silence bothered him. After making sure his Colt was loose in the holster, he stepped up on to the veranda and lifted the knocker next to the door.

He was about to knock again when he heard someone coming. The door opened and he found himself looking into the business end of a pistol.

'Oh, Cordy, I'm sorry,' Hannah stammered, quickly lowering the gun. 'I should have looked out the window before opening the door, but. . . .' She let the sentence fade out.

Cordy chuckled. 'No harm done. At least you didn't pull the trigger. It is loaded, isn't it?'

'Yes. And if you'd been anyone else I might have been quicker, too. Oh, I'm so glad you're back.'

'Where is everyone? It's quiet as a Sunday.'

'Father's in his room at the back of the house and he more than likely didn't hear you knock. I was in the kitchen. Say, I've got a fresh pot of coffee on the stove. Would you like a cup?'

'I sure would. I ran out this morning, but all I've been drinking is camp coffee anyway. A good cup would go good right now. Let me get my saddlebags.'

Following her through the house and into the kitchen was a pleasure. He liked the way her body moved and felt his face flush as he watched her walk ahead of him.

'Carl and Caleb have been taking turns, kind of standing guard during the day down by the front gate. At night they stay closer, keeping watch from up in the barn.'

'Why would they be doing that? Has something happened while I was gone?'

'Yes. Well, nothing really, but Carl wanted

to go out and work on the fence, so they rode out the day you left,' she said, taking the steaming pot from the back of the shiny black wood stove and pouring two cups.

'They were pretty happy about the amount of fencing they got up when they came in that night. They had worked all day and looked it. That night someone came along and pulled down all the posts they'd put in. They rode back in before noon, figuring it wouldn't do any good to fight it. Anything they'd do would just get undone. It was Bosewell's blasted foreman who caused the trouble this time. He and a couple men from the B-Bar-B, not his cowhands but Caleb said they were his gunmen, rode in a day or two later, laughing and joking about Carl and Caleb giving up. They were taunting Caleb a lot, about how he was getting too big for his britches, trying to be a hand on a real ranch again when everyone knew he was nothing but a saloon bum. I used Father's rifle and fired over their heads. They rode out laughing, saying they'd be back. That's when Carl thought it'd be a good idea to set up a watch.'

Cordy sipped his coffee and frowned. 'Yeah, I've met that Price once before.' Then he held up a hand before the girl could ask about it. 'But never mind about that. Can you get your father out here?' He brought the saddlebags up and started unbuckling their flaps. 'I've got some good news here, I think.'

CHAPTER FOURTEEN

Zach Colfield wheeled himself into the kitchen in answer to his daughter's call.

'Well, boy, it's good to see you.' Cordy heard that the man's voice wasn't as weak sounding as he'd first thought. The man was just soft-spoken. 'Hannah has been spending a lot of her time watching out the kitchen window, expecting to see you ride in at any time.'

'Father, I did not,' she quickly responded, blushing. Cordy hid his smile by turning to the saddlebags.

'Well, I got what I went after,' he said, bringing out a handful of the yellow metal.

'Oh, my,' both father and daughter

exclaimed, their eyes fixed on the gold. For a long moment neither could say a thing.

'I don't know how much is here,' said Cordy, wanting to fill the silence, 'or how much it'll take to satisfy your note at the bank, but I figure there's enough to give you some breathing room, at least.'

'Well, I don't know what to say, young man. I suppose it would be bad manners to ask the source of this treasure, wouldn't it?'

Cordy nodded, pursing his lips. 'I came by it honestly, that's all that matters. It's raw gold taken from a place quite a ways up in the high country. A couple old-timers found the place and for a while the three of us worked it, taking only what was needed. One of them is now dead and the other is somewhere down along the border country, spending his last years sitting in the sun. I don't think they'd care if I took out enough to get your ranch out of trouble. But I suppose the best thing to do would be to take this into Silver Canyon and to the bank. Carrying around raw gold makes me kinda nervous.'

*

Carl and Caleb welcomed Cordy when they came in that evening. Carl appeared to be his normal self, but Caleb had obviously been in a fight.

'Hey, what happened?' asked Cordy, seeing a half-healed cut on his chin and the deep-purple discoloring around his right eye.

'Those blamed gunmen riding with Price think they're so blasted smart,' Carl snarled as he stripped the saddle from his horse. 'And Caleb here ain't much smarter, I'll tell you.'

'C'mon, old man,' Caleb cut in, waving a hand toward Cordy. 'It wasn't so much.'

'Yeah? Well, let me tell you, it sometimes pays off to keep your mouth shut.'

'That's enough bickering between the two of you,' Hannah ordered. 'I didn't want to tell you, Cordy. I wasn't sure how you'd react.'

'So, what happened?'

'Well,' Caleb started, only to be interrupted by Carl. It was clear to Cordy that the two men had become saddle partners in the brief time they'd been riding together.

'Let me tell it so he gets the full picture. We were out working on the fence, a day or two after you rode off. Where did you go, anyway? We coulda used your help, you know.'

'Never mind that, go on with your story.'

'We were out there when that blamed Price and four or five of his men come riding up. His gunmen put us under their weapons while a couple of them started roping the posts we'd just put in, pulling them down. While that was going on, Price climbed off that big horse he rides and started yammering at Caleb here, calling him all kinds of names. Of course Caleb wasn't smart enough to let it roll over him, no, sir. He had to step up and throw a punch at the man. Don't pay any attention to the hardcases just a setting there pointing their Colts at us. Well, you can see what happened. That blamed Price worked Caleb over pretty good. In the end Caleb had had enough and didn't get up. Or couldn't get up. Price told me not to bother fixing any more of the fence. Said he didn't want to waste his time, coming out to tear it up. Then, laughing like a bunch of hyenas, they rode off.'

'I been beat before and a lot worse than this,' Caleb grumbled. He stepped over to dunk his head in a water trough.

'There wasn't anything we could do after that, Cordy, except stick closer to the ranch. That's what you said to do, but we didn't listen at first.'

'OK, there isn't much to be done about that fence now anyway. Tomorrow we'll take the buggy for Mr Colfield and ride into town. Be wearing your gunbelt.'

CHAPTER FIFTEEN

There wasn't much discussion on the ride into town the next morning. Even during the breakfast that Hannah had set out, with all four of them sitting around the big table in the kitchen, nobody seemed to have much to say. Now, with Colfield and his daughter in the buggy going on ahead, the man's wheelchair tied to the back, and the three men riding along behind, little was said.

Cordy, bringing up the rear of the little parade, was giving things a lot of study. He knew that anyone looking at the way things were going might question how he'd got himself so involved. Somehow it just seemed natural. From the moment he'd braced Bosewell and his three or four men in the front yard of the Boxed C to now, riding in to pay off a bank loan, he'd felt it was the right thing to do.

It did bother him a little, using what he considered to be someone else's gold to help out the Colfields, but he figured that both Cletus and Zeb wouldn't mind if they knew. And riding in to support the rancher and his daughter was what he'd been hired to do, wasn't it? When a rannie hired on, he rode for the brand. It was as simple as that. Looking ahead at the buggy carrying Hannah and her pa he knew it wasn't as simple as that, though. He had to shake his head. Anything that had to do with the young woman wasn't even close to being simple.

As they came into town all three men paid close attention to things. It wouldn't surprise anyone if Bosewell or some of his men didn't make some effort to cause trouble. Paying off that loan certainly wouldn't please the greedy horse-breeder. Traffic on the main street didn't look to be anything but what could be expected for a mid-week working day. Several horses were tied to hitch rails in front of businesses, along with a couple wagons and buggies. People, mostly men, Cordy noted, were either standing on the plank boardwalks on each side or walking from one place to another. Nobody appeared to pay the Colfield cavalcade any notice.

While Caleb dropped the lead tied to the halter on the buggy's horse over a railing, Carl and Cordy lifted the wheelchair onto the boardwalk, then helped Zach Colfield into it. Settled in, and smiling, the rancher nodded his thanks and wheeled himself through the bank's door.

'Well, Zach Colfield,' the short pot-bellied man called out as he pushed through the railing to come forward to take the wheelchair-bound man's hand. 'It's been some time since we've had the pleasure of your company, man. How is everything out at the Boxed C?'

'Boys,' Colfield glanced over his shoulder at his three hired hands, 'this here is Matt Blankenship, owner of the bank, a member of the city council and one of the most important men in the basin. Matt, you know my daughter, Hannah, and of course you'd know Carl. The other two are working for me. Caleb you've probably seen around town, and the stranger is Cordy Lowell.'

'Well, yes,' the banker stood dry-washing his hands as his eyes flicked from one person to another. 'I'd heard you'd been looking for men. It's too bad that you're only been able to find so few. Making a herd will be hard work for the three you have.'

'That's true. But we'll manage. Now let's get on to business.'

'Ah, yes. The loan the bank made you, for fencing wasn't it? I'd have to check, but I seem to recall that the note is coming due in the next few days, isn't it?'

'Matt,' Colfield said with a chuckle, 'don't try to tell me you don't know to the exact minute that note is due and payable.'

Blankenship grimaced, then, seeing how only the rancher was laughing and the others were standing unsmiling at him, he let his frown deepen.

'Well, yes, yes. I guess that's true. Now,' the banker hurried on, 'I hate to tell you, but the way things are, well, I'm afraid I won't be able to extend that note, much as I'd like to. It just wouldn't be good business, I'm sure you can appreciate that.'

Colfield sat silently for a minute, nodding his understanding. 'Yeah, I didn't expect anything else, Matt. I certainly didn't.'

Cordy nearly laughed out loud at the obvious relief that the banker felt.

'But that's not what we're here for today,' Colfield went on. He held out Cordy's saddlebags. 'I'd like you to weigh out the gold specie here. I think you'll find there's enough to cover the note and a goodly sum left over. Your bank acts as an official assayer, doesn't it?'

'What? Gold? Why, yes, yes, of course.' Being handed gold flustered the banker. Glancing at Hannah, Cordy saw her smile at the banker's distress; it clearly wasn't what Blankenship had expected.

'Well, get going then, man. Don't just stand there,' said Colfield, no longer smiling or laughing but now all business.

'Yes, yes.' Blankenship, holding the saddlebags as if holding a rattlesnake, looked around, then called to a clerk. 'Harris will take care of this. It'll take a few minutes. If you'd like to go take care of any shopping you may want to do, we'll have it all done by the time you get back.'

Colfield shook his head. 'No, Matt. We'll stay right here and watch.'

Colfield wheeled himself closer to the railing and he and Hannah took up their positions to wait and watch. Cordy and the others nodded to the rancher, then tepped back out to stand on the boardwalk.

'Boy, that banker didn't know whether to fish or cut bait, did he?' Caleb laughed.

'I don't think he liked it much. He was enjoying the idea of being able to turn down Mr Colfield too much.'

Carl, looking lazily up and down the street, nodded. 'Way back before that blamed fool

Bosewell came into the basin, Blankenship was pretty friendly with all the ranchers and farmers in the area. Since the B-Bar-B started growing he's tied his bank onto that outfit, leaving all the others to fend for themselves. Can't blame him, I suppose. Most of the businesses here in Silver Canyon have done the same.'

Cordy shook his head. 'Wonder what would happen if someone else came in and knocked that Bosewell down a peg or two?'

'That ain't likely to happen,' Caleb said, 'not while he's got all the clout. I doubt anyone could stand up to Price. And then there's all those gunhands taking Bosewell's money.'

'Well, you never know,' was all Cordy could say.

Moments later Colfield and Hannah pushed through the bank door.

'Here, Cordy,' Colfield said, handing the young cowhand a little booklet. 'There was a good amount of money left over after paying off my note and I had Blankenship put it in an account with your name on it. You're now are a man of means.' Not giving anyone a chance to comment, he went on, 'Hannah and I have some business down the street, so if you boys want to go have a drink or a cup of coffee, we'll come looking for you when we're finished.' He turned his wheelchair away and the two of them left the three men.

'Boy, that sure made a world of difference in the old man. Paying off that note took away a lot of stress. I wonder what he's up to now?' Carl asked. He shook his head before going on: 'Well, Caleb, you heard him. Our young friend here has money in the bank. I figure that to celebrate he should buy the first round of drinks.'

CHAPTER SIXTEEN

The saloon was nearly empty when the three bellied up to the long mahogany bar. Standing in the cool dimness of the long room, they quietly talked while sipping the foamy beer.

'Well, I never did hear where that gold came from,' Carl mumbled, careful to keep his eyes down, not looking at Cordy or Caleb for an answer.

'I wonder,' Caleb mused when the young cowboy didn't respond, 'now that the pressure of an overdue loan is gone, what Bosewell will pull next.'

Cordy sipped his beer, wiping the foam

from his upper lip, and didn't say anything. Thinking back to the Indian he'd killed, he wondered how he was going to deal with Price. He brushed a hand over his shirt front; he believed he could feel the burning of the brand on his chest. All he could remember of the man, Price, was the sound of his foul-mouthed language as he gave the orders to put his mark on the boy they had caught. That boy, Cordy knew, had grown up. But would it be enough?

'Well, that's enough daydreaming, boys,' Carl said, putting his empty glass down on the bar. 'Let's go see what the boss wants to do. We spend too much more time here in town and it'll be dark by the time we get back to the home place.'

The others nodded their agreement and followed him back out into the sunshine. Seeing the Colfields standing near the buggy, they crossed the street.

'Well, looky here,' a loud blustery voice carried down the street. 'If it ain't most everyone from the Boxed C. Come to town to beg for another loan, are ya?'

Everyone turned to see Bosewell followed by half a dozen men come striding down the center of the street.

Colfield didn't respond, just continued to sit in this chair with Hannah standing to one side.

'Heard tell you was in town, Colfield,' Bosewell called out. He came up and stood with his hands on his hips, his feet apart. Standing as he was, Cordy thought he resembled a thick tree-trunk wearing a dark-wool suit, a wide-brimmed hat sitting squarely on his block-shaped head. 'What are you doing, getting ready to leave the basin? Old Blankenship wouldn't sell me your note, but that don't matter. Too bad you ain't been able to hire enough men to make a round-up. Guess that means I'll be getting the Boxed C before long, don't it? Your own damn fault it had to turn out like this. I warned you to accept my price a while back. Too bad I can't say your place is worth that much any more.'

His men, all wearing tied-down holstered

revolvers and a couple holding their rifles in the crooks of their arms, had spread out in a line now, facing Colfield and the Boxed C men.

'Well, what do you got to say for yourself, Colfield?'

'Nothing. I've nothing to say to you, Bosewell. Oh, except you can stop waiting for the bank to foreclose on my note. I just paid it off.'

'What?' Bosewell stepped back a step. 'Where'n hell would you find the money to do that?' He glanced at Cordy and sneered. 'Unless this stranger here gave it to you. Looking at him, I'd say he doesn't look like he'd have two dollars to rub together, but I did hear a story a while back about his having some gold. Wonder where you'd get enough gold, boy? Ain't heard of any banks or stagecoaches being robbed lately.' Laughing at his own joke, the horse-breeder glanced to make sure his men were laughing with him.

Feeling his face flush at being talked about like that, Cordy took a couple steps closer to the short, squat man. He thumbed the thong off his Colt, stopped and looked over the men standing beside the loud-mouthed rancher.

'Boys, as I recall, it's nearing the end of the month. Now that likely means you haven't been paid yet this month. Anyone does any talking they can't back up or pulls a pistol to back up such a loud mouth should give it a thought. I'll get the first shot off and it'll be centered at your fat boss. Who'll pay you then?'

'What? Who you calling fat?'

'Why, you. I'd like an apology for your suggesting any money I may have was stolen. I don't take that kind of talk from anyone, leastways, not from a short, fat loudmouth like you.'

'Hey, there, boy,' someone called from the plank walkway behind Cordy, 'I'd be a little careful, was I you, calling Mr Bosewell names like that.'

Cordy glanced at the man. He felt his body heat up. Without thinking his left hand swept across the burning of his chest. Hesitating only long enough to think about it, he shook his head and turned back to face the blocky horse-breeder.

'Nope. As I said, any trouble and my first bullet goes to your Mr Bosewell.'

'Hey, wait a minute. You go pulling iron on me and you're dead. Look around you, boy, there's a dozen guns just waiting to put you down.'

'Uh huh, but you won't see it happen. You'll already be in the dirt. Now, about that apology.' Cordy stood, his shoulders square, his right hand resting on the cedar butt of his Colt.

For a long moment nobody spoke, then someone levered a shell into his rifle, the sound cutting through the morning quiet.

'I figure to back up my partner,' Carl said, letting his words carry down the street. Glancing quickly over his shoulder, Cordy saw the man standing with his rifle ready to fire. Caleb, a cold smile on his face, reached over and pulled his rifle from the saddle scabbard.

'Yep. Just in case old Cordy here might

miss, I reckon neither Carl nor I will. It'll be you first, Bosewell.'

Slowly, one at a time, the men closest to the rancher stepped away until he was standing alone. Looking first one way and then the other, panic crossed Bosewell's face. It faded when a big, wide-shouldered man stepped over to his side.

'I knew I could count on you, Price. The rest of you,' he called out, 'can ride. And don't be hanging around looking to get paid any more. You're all done with the B-Bar-B.'

Cordy chuckled without humor. 'You'd be Price, wouldn't you?' he asked. He glanced at the big man stepping of the boardwalk and into the street. He recognized the man. It was the permanent sneering smile that brought back that morning. The scar, a white worm of a mark cutting across his cheek was seared in Cordy's brain. Cordy felt himself go cold.

'Yeah, I'm Price,' the gunman scoffed. 'I knew we'd have to meet up sooner or later, what with you causing the boss so much trouble. And I gotta tell ya, somehow your warning to shoot the boss doesn't scare me much. I don't think you're man enough to do it.'

'Oh, I'm man enough. Unlike you, I always do my own dirty work. But tell me, Price, who are you going to get to do your branding for you? That Indian partner of yours won't be putting the hot iron to anyone any more.'

'What about the Indian?' asked Bosewell quickly.

'Oh, he's gone on to the happy hunting ground. You did know about the branding he and this bully boy of yours did for you, didn't you? Going around putting your brand on men. You should have known. Yeah, it seems Price likes to have his mark put on people and that Indian liked doing it. Well, Price, guess you'll have to find someone else to do your dirty work. The Indian won't be coming home.'

Bosewell didn't like that. 'I don't know anything about that.'

Cordy, not taking his eyes off the two men, snorted disgustedly. 'Nope, of course you don't. Hells bells, anyone can see you're an honest man. But that makes me wonder just how honest are you? Take that stud horse of yours. I hear it's a big light gray dun with stripes of black running down its back and a scattering of Appaloosa spots on its rump. Sure sounds to me to be a lot like the horse Price here stole from me a few years back. Put my brand on it, he told the Indian, then changed his mind and had the ranch brand burned into its rump. Oh, yeah, Price, we've met before. You likely wouldn't remember, but I do. Tell me, Bosewell, you have a bill of sale for that dun horse you're so proud of?'

Seeing the man's face blanch, Cordy laughed. 'Wonder what the courts down in Denver will say when that question gets asked?'

'Damn you,' Price snarled, and let his hand drop to his gun butt.

'I wouldn't, Price,' Caleb yelled coldly. 'I still hurt from that beating you gave me and I'd like nothing better than to lay you out.'

'You can't prove a word of it,' Bosewell

snarled. 'All I've heard are words. That dun is mine. It carries my brand and that's the end of it.'

'That's not exactly true, Bosewell,' Caleb answered loudly. 'I was there when what Cordy here said happened. Price had just killed two men he claimed were rustlers by letting No-nose John put the ranch brand on them. As I recall, a kid came riding up and Price had the Indian put his own brand on him and the ranch brand on the kid's horse. It was a dun, just like he says, like the one that's been making you rich.'

'Naw, that ain't no proof.'

Feeling the heat coming from his chest was more than Cordy could stand. He reached up with his left hand, pulled at his shirt, popping the buttons and exposing on his chest the welts of the brand: the letter P with a line through the upper part. The Slash P.

'Oh, my God,' he heard Hannah exclaim.

'Why, you young whelp,' Price snarled, pulling at his six-gun.

Without thinking about it, in a single

motion Cordy lifted his Colt, hit the hammer with the heel of his left hand and fired three shots. For a brief second the big man stood, expressionless, his shoulders slowly slumping before he folded face down in the dust of the street.

Focusing on Price, Cordy didn't hear other shots being fired and was surprised to see Bosewell lying out flat on his back, a small silver pistol clutched in one hand.

CHAPTER SEVENTEEN

There were more witnesses to the shooting than Sheriff Claude Dallas needed. With Bosewell dead and all the gunmen he had hired gone, the sheriff was just the first to realize that things had changed in the basin. Calling the shooting self-defense, he got a few men to carry the two bodies over to the undertaker's and declared the matter closed.

Colfield waited until Cordy had been over to the general store to replace the shirt he'd torn off himself before meeting with everyone at the hotel restaurant.

'Boy,' the rancher said once the waitress had brought them all coffee. 'This turned out differently from what I thought it would. I wasn't sure what would happen when Bosewell found out we'd paid off that note but I couldn't have foreseen this happening.'

Cordy, in his new shirt, sat with his head down, staring into the steaming cup in front of him.

'And that brings me to something else,' Colfield went on. 'Cordy, while you, Carl and Caleb were waiting for us, Hannah and I visited the attorney. I figured the gold that you came up with did more than just pay off my loan. It also bought you half-interest in the ranch. Boys,' he glanced at Carl and Caleb, 'shake hands with your new boss.'

Laughing, both men reached across to take Cordy's hand, ignoring his blank look.

'There's something else for you to think about, too,' said Hannah, taking the hand they had been shaking. 'From what Caleb said and that mark on your chest, I think you could make a good case in court about the ownership of that dun horse that Bosewell has used for his breeding program. Fact is, I wouldn't be surprised if you could make a legal case for ownership of all the offspring of that horse.'

Cordy sat for a long moment thinking about what had happened. For the first time he couldn't feel the brand on his chest and nobody had looked at him any differently since they'd seen it. Maybe there wasn't any shame in it after all. And now he was part-owner in a ranch and maybe more than that.

'You know,' he said slowly, 'it all goes back to two men, Cletus and Zeb. It was the gold they had found that I went to get to pay off the loan. They were the ones who saved me and helped me grow up. They're the ones I have to thank.'

'Tell me about this Zeb,' Hannah said. 'Father, wasn't your younger brother named Zebulon? Didn't you say he went off hunting for gold? I wonder if he's the Zeb that Cordy is talking about.'

'Well, if he is, then for certain the gold he found has come home.' He glanced down at the hand that his daughter still held and went on, 'and it's brought us a new member of the family at the same time. A man couldn't ask for more than that, could he?'